The Summer Request

A N J
P r e s s

THE SUMMER REQUEST

ANJ Press, First edition. MAY 2022.

Copyright © 2022 Amelia Addler.

Written by Amelia Addler.

Cover design by CrocoDesigns

Maps by MistyBeee

For the promise of youth and the wisdom of friends

May 17th, 2022

J ustine Emerald's life ended on an island.

Connected to the mainland by a single two-lane road, Mount Desert Island gracefully breaks from Maine's coast and rises from the sea with plumes of dense forests and mountain giants dressed in pink granite. Distinct from the generic calendar-like charm of a tropical island, Mount Desert has its own rugged, picturesque beauty with miles of rocky coastlines, rolling meadows, and crystal-clear lakes.

Nearly half of the island is a national park – Acadia, one of the smallest and most visited in the country. A mecca for hiking, kayaking, rock climbing, and lobster eating, the island is its own kind of paradise, and as good as anywhere to die.

Were Justine able to spring back from the dead in a fantastical Justine-like way, she would delight in the morbid fact that both her entry and exit from life occurred on islands.

Born Justine Miller 2,231 nautical miles from Mount Desert, she burst into the world with little warning. Her mother's precipitous labor proved to be a poetic foreshadowing. Poor Tammy Miller wasn't ready to be a mother – not then, perhaps not ever. She'd only managed to don one shoe before giving birth in the hallway of her small San Juan Island home, a fact Justine was never allowed to forget.

Justine loved growing up on San Juan Island. Set off the coast of Washington state, it's one of over a hundred islands that make up the charming archipelago known as the San Juan Islands. Picturesque and wild, the islands allowed her to explore seemingly endless beaches, wildflower-covered hill-tops, and stoic lighthouses.

When she tried to make Mount Desert Island her home, Justine focused on the similarities to San Juan – the evergreen trees, the craggy coastlines, and the breathtaking views. She was trying to make her husband happy, after all, and he preferred Maine to Washington.

However, the differences between the islands were stark.

The San Juan Islands live under the grace of the Olympic and Vancouver Island mountains' rain shadow, resulting in temperate and calm weather that rarely dips below freezing, unlike snow-ridden Maine.

The islands are kept wild, with no roads connecting any of the San Juan Islands to the mainland. The four largest islands are accessible by public ferry, but the rest are reachable only by private air or watercraft.

Beyond the seclusion, the ecosystem of San Juan proved impossible to imitate. One of her greatest loves had been the wildlife of the surrounding Salish Sea, brimming with harbor seals, porpoises, humpbacks, and her favorite: orcas.

Whenever life knocked her down, she'd retreat to the park on the west side of San Juan Island and watch as bald eagles flew overhead, so common they bored her, and wait for the sleek black and white whales to mill past.

It never got old – their tall fins slicing through the water, their powerful breaths blasting a hundred feet from shore. The sight always filled her with awe, making her feel like she had a place in this beautiful, crazy world.

The whales had a tradition of returning to the islands each summer, following the runs of salmon, much as the Coast Salish people had done for generations. Justine had planned that she, too, would make a custom of returning each summer, because try as she might – as beautiful as Mount Desert was – it simply wasn't home.

Yet, on that cool evening in May, Justine met her end and her tiny tradition was destroyed. It was nothing compared to the Coast Salish people being forced off of their lands, or even to the orcas being starved of their salmon, but to a certain few, it was a catastrophe.

Righting that ship took no small effort, and the hours and days following her untimely death were filled dotting the T's and crossing the I's on a hastily sealed non-disclosure agreement that firmly shut the door on the truth.

It was only in silence that Justine could be cremated, packed into a shining walnut box, and sent home to her beloved San Juan Island for the last time.

THE SAN JUAN ISLANDS

One

I t seemed odd for Justine's memorial to be held in Roche Harbor. They'd hardly spent any time there when they were growing up. If they'd ever tried to bring their mischief to the community, they'd instantly be chased off by a shopkeeper or restaurant owner who didn't want their paying tourists disturbed by a group of shrieking girls.

Michelle squinted into the sun as she counted the people in attendance. There were only twenty-three so far. The service was going to start in half an hour. Where was everyone? Where were Justine's famous friends, where were her dedicated followers? Perhaps there had been a more exclusive service on the mainland.

That would make sense. San Juan Island wasn't the easiest to get to, a common complaint from Justine's ex-husband Lou. Michelle always wondered if that was the real reason Justine had never moved back, or if there was more to it. Now she'd never know.

The thought drifted and settled heavily onto her chest. *Never* was the reality of death, though the *nevers* don't make themselves known all at once. Loss was strange like that.

Harsh realizations cropped up randomly, each *never* piling onto the last and leaving an impenetrable feeling of unease.

She cleared her throat and looked around again. Surely their old high school friends would find a way to make it? Of their group, Michelle was the only one who still lived on San Juan. Her three other friends, including Justine, had fled as soon as they could because, like any wonderful place to grow up, San Juan was safe and therefore boring.

Michelle wasn't sure if Lisa or Valerie were coming to the memorial. She'd called them both when she heard about Justine's death. Valerie had missed the call, and when she'd returned it, Michelle was too busy to answer. Lisa had answered but couldn't talk long, and the result was a series of texts that fizzled out without ever confirming their plans.

That was, unfortunately, how many of their conversations went these days. Michelle told herself it might be better if they didn't come. It'd been years since they'd spent any substantial time together, and as the summer picked up steam, the island was being overtaken by tourists.

It wouldn't be any fun for them to visit now. It wouldn't be like old times, not really, and Michelle wasn't in the mood to entertain. Tourists were good for her business, but bad for her nerves. She preferred the peace of the winter, strolling along a pebbly beach and taking solace in the fact she was the only living soul there.

None of this was good for her nerves, actually. Her chair was sinking into the ground. It was an elegant little thing, white wood draped in some shimmery material, but it was better suited for a wedding, not a memorial in a garden by the sea. Her back hurt already.

She stood to get a drink and survey the space. It was a lovely day, sunny but not too warm, with a slight breeze from the ocean. Along the sides of the white picket fence hung hundreds of fresh-cut flowers, and a delicate, decorative fabric hung over Justine's enormous picture. The bottom was knotted in flowers somehow, and it blew in the breeze, capturing her attention for a moment.

Someone had clearly gone to great lengths to make this memorial beautiful. It couldn't have been Justine's ex-husband. He wasn't even here.

It may have been one of his many minions. Whoever they were, they'd thought it was a good idea to serve refreshments and hors d'oeuvres, which was all very nice until it attracted the wrong sort of people.

Funeral crashers.

It was bound to happen. Michelle knew what people were like.

She turned her attention to diligently studying the faces of every person entering the little garden. There were a few she recognized, but many she didn't. Her and Justine's lives were not as close as they once were. When they were young, they had known all the same people, and the most excitement they'd had was sneaking into the lagoon to skinny dip.

She smiled to herself.

"Excuse me?"

Michelle turned to see an unfamiliar man standing behind her. She forced a smile, unsure if she was supposed to recognize him. "Hi."

He leaned forward, dropping his voice. "Would you mind adding a little something to my lemonade?" He winked. "Hard to get by without it, you know?"

Michelle took a step back. "I'm sorry?"

He sighed and the twinkle disappeared from his eye. "Do you have vodka? I'll even settle for gin."

Ah, right. He assumed she worked there. Was it because of her outfit? She'd worn a dark dress, the only one she had. She didn't think it made her look *that* much like a member of the waitstaff.

Probably a funeral crasher.

"I don't work here," she said flatly, walking off with a glass of seltzer water.

"Oh, sorry," he called out, lacking any hint of embarrassment.

Michelle took her seat again and fidgeted with the hem of her dress. Perhaps it wasn't as nice as she thought it was? She hadn't worn it in years and was just relieved it still fit. She hadn't put much effort into her outfit. The shock of Justine's passing had completely filled her thoughts.

Laughs and loud voices rumbled behind her, and she turned to see Lou making his entrance, a beautiful young woman on his arm. Michelle stared, making a count of how many of the unfamiliar mourners greeted them, laughing and shaking hands.

Oh, dear old Lou. How nice it must be to have friends wherever he went.

A man tapped her on the shoulder, asking if the seat next to her was taken. She shook her head, and he picked the chair up and walked off, leaving Michelle with the growing realization that she was the only person from Justine's old life who had made it to the service.

"All right, Louis, you're blocking the entire walkway," griped a voice from behind.

Michelle knew who it was without having to look – Justine's mother, her voice raspy from decades of smoking.

"Last I checked you weren't the king of England, so why don't you find yourself a seat?"

Michelle watched as Tammy Miller pushed her way through before taking a seat in the front row.

She suppressed a smile. While she and Mrs. Miller certainly weren't friends, Michelle still enjoyed it when someone else bore the brunt of the old woman's temper.

Mrs. Miller caught her eye and offered a curt nod. Michelle nodded back.

It was nice not to be alone.

Two

The ferry was just as she remembered it. Was it possible they hadn't gotten new ships in the last fifteen years? Or did ferries only come in one design, already perfected, with no need to be improved?

Lisa adored the Washington State ferries, and she loved it whenever she got a chance to step away from her everyday life and go for a ride. Even when stuck on dry land, she loved watching the green and white ships break over the horizon, forever a symbol of adventure and the vastness of the world.

Nothing else in life could pull off that bold green and white. Once, in a fit of nostalgia, she tried to paint their family room that exact shade of ferry green. It was a miserable failure, and her son had forever dubbed the space The Kermit Room.

It felt good to be on a ship again. One change she did notice, however, was the car fee. Who could afford it? Lisa had panicked a little when she'd arrived at the ferry terminal in Anacortes and tried to buy a ticket.

She had to make the quick decision to leave her car on the mainland and walk onto the ferry. At some point during the hour-long trip, she'd figure out how to catch a ride to Roche Harbor for the memorial.

Lisa found herself a seat inside with a view of the water. The smells from the galley were tempting – soft pretzels, pizza, and were those curly fries?

No. She didn't need anything else. She'd packed a peanut butter and jelly sandwich, and that was enough. If she'd had a traveling companion, they could've split a bottle of wine as they gazed out onto the passing islands, the brilliant blue sky and blinding white clouds barely floating by...

Lisa let out a sigh and got up to throw out the foil from her sandwich. As enchanting as ferry travel could be, she was traveling alone today.

She stepped onto the deck outside and found a spot to hang her hands over the railing. The boat slowly but steadily hummed its way across the water, past one island and onto the next.

She'd never appreciated the views when she was younger. All she could think of was how inconvenient it was to have to take a boat every time she wanted to go somewhere. Her parents had laughed and patted her head knowingly, telling her that she should enjoy island time.

Lisa hadn't cared about that. She'd just wanted to be able to go to the mall like a regular teenager.

Back then, she couldn't wait to get away from the island and live where all the action was. City life did end up being more exciting, and more convenient, though now she'd determined that convenience wasn't always a good thing.

An announcement came over the loudspeakers, stating they were approaching Friday Harbor on San Juan Island. Lisa was cutting it close. The ferry had been late, and now she had to figure out how to get a ride. Surely Uber had made its way to San Juan Island?

Within a few minutes of docking, she had her answer. Uber had not made it, and the bus she'd hoped to catch to the other side of the island had just left. It wouldn't be back for another forty-five minutes.

Island time struck again.

Lisa stood on the sidewalk of Front Street, and though she tried to focus on her predicament, she kept getting distracted by what she saw. So much had changed, yet it still looked the same.

The buildings were familiar, in a way. Many were the same structures that had been built in 1900, standing now as they had then. Lisa used to think that was boring, but now it amazed her.

Though the buildings were in the same location, they looked brand new. New paint, new siding, gorgeous windows. It made the street look like something out of a Hallmark movie. All of the restaurants and shops of her childhood had disappeared, only to be replaced by new ventures. Some looked positively chic.

The Friday Harbor of her youth had not been chic. She couldn't go far without running into a group of fishermen having an end-of-the-day beer. Years later, any fishy stench could thrust her into a sentimental spiral.

A car honked, startling her out of her thoughts.

"Lisa?"

A woman had stopped traffic, rolling her window down to get Lisa's attention.

"Hi, yes," Lisa said, stumbling closer.

"I'm Zora, Justine's assistant." She looked down. "I'm sorry, her previous assistant."

"Of course." Lisa would've recognized her if she hadn't had her head in the clouds. "We've met before. How are you?"

"Good." Zora nodded. "I thought I would swing by and pick up any stragglers from the ferry. Have you seen anyone else who looks like they're trying to get to the memorial?"

Lisa was too embarrassed to admit she hadn't done anything but gape at the buildings. "I can't say I have."

Zora thought on that for a moment. "Okay. Would you like a ride?"

"Yes! Thank you," Lisa said, grabbing at the back door and launching herself inside. There was no need to further upset the line of cars forming behind them by being slow. "I really appreciate it."

In her rush, Lisa realized she was treating Zora, Justine's loyal assistant of over twenty-five years, like a cab driver.

As soon as she shut the car door, she tried to correct herself. "Sorry I got in the back seat," Lisa announced. "I think I panicked. There were cars waiting and I'm so used to the city, where people are angry all the time."

Zora waved a hand. "Don't worry about it. Not at all. I'm just glad you made it."

"Me too." Lisa smiled. To think she almost hadn't.

Zora drove through town slowly, stopping for pedestrians at every corner. The streets were filled with happy families and couples, the sun illuminating their smiling faces.

"Did you just get to the island today?" Lisa asked.

"No, I arrived last week. I've been busy planning the memorial and getting things in order. Justine designated me the executor of her estate. I need to talk to you later, actually. You, Michelle, and Valerie."

Lisa raised an eyebrow, but didn't ask any questions. "No problem."

To Lisa's slight disappointment, Zora took the most direct route to Roche Harbor. It was the sensible thing to do, but her favorite route was more scenic, with glimpses of the ocean through trees and past rocky bluffs. She wouldn't be on the island long and wanted to enjoy the short time she had. Her car was probably getting a ticket as she sat there, daydreaming.

The last time she'd been on the island was when her mom had passed away. Life had gotten too busy, between the kids and work, and she'd never had a moment to sit down. It seemed like she was always telling herself things would slow down after this, or that, or the next thing. It never did.

"The weather is perfect here," Zora said as she took a curve a little too quickly. "Justine always talked about it being perfect, but now I really get it."

Another benefit over Seattle. Lisa leaned forward. "Yeah. Justine was right."

They arrived at the memorial with a few minutes to spare. Zora disappeared and Lisa debated if she should grab a snack before sitting down.

Before she could make up her mind, Michelle called out to her.

"Lisa!"

She beamed. "Shell!"

Michelle looked as beautiful as ever. She had a few wrinkles and a whisper of gray hair, but her skin was as dewy as ever, and she looked toned and fit in her understated black dress.

What did people think when they looked at Lisa? Probably that she was fatter than they'd remembered. That's what Lisa thought every time she caught herself in a mirror, or saw a picture of herself. *So many bad angles,* she'd laugh.

Not that Michelle would agree. She was always kind.

Lisa pulled her in for a hug. "It's so good to see you."

"You too. I'm glad you could make it. You look great!"

Lisa shook her head. "Don't start lying to me now, Shell. I've somehow turned into one of my mother's frumpy hats."

"You have not," Michelle said firmly.

But she had. Lisa knew it was true. It bothered her, of course it did, but there are more important things in life. She was thinking of trying Weight Watchers again, and her daughter kept nagging her to go shopping for a new wardrobe.

A new wardrobe would be a bit much. She could maybe agree to buying a few key staples.

Michelle spoke again. "Have you heard from Valerie?"

Lisa snapped her attention back to Michelle. This memorial was beautifully done. That Zora was an expert. "I talked to her, and she said she'd try to make it. I'm sure she'll be here."

"Are you?" Michelle asked, a half-smile on her face.

Just then, the sound of a helicopter approaching filled their ears.

Lisa pointed up. "I'll bet you a doughnut Val's on that helicopter."

Three

The pilot landed and yelled at her through the headset. "You've gotta go. I'm running late."

"Not until the blade stops spinning," Val said, shaking her head. "It'll mess up my hair."

She carefully removed her headset, missing his grumbling response.

It wouldn't kill him to wait one more minute. She pulled a mirror out of her purse and fixed her hair before dabbing on a touch of lipstick.

When it seemed safe, Val made a dainty exit from the helicopter and slammed the door behind her. She shimmied to the grassy garden, awkwardly trying to keep her heels from sinking into the ground.

The memorial was fenced off and looked like something out of a dream. There must have been thousands of flowers between the fence, the chairs, and Justine's picture. *How elegant.*

Val spotted her old friends staring at her and rushed to greet them.

"Valerie Villano," Lisa said, shaking her head. "You had to make an entrance, didn't you?"

"Oh, that?" She kissed Lisa gingerly on the cheek. "It's the only way to travel. Don't tell me you drove?"

"I took the scenic route," Lisa said. "It involved a car, and a boat, and another car...no helicopter for me, though. I'm no celebrity."

Val laughed. It was fun to tease, and be teased by, Lisa again. "I assume my route was scenic, though I didn't look down much."

"It's good to see you." Michelle gave her a hug. "I think they're getting started soon."

"Of course," Val said, her voice hushed.

They took their seats and moments later, the music grew louder. Val tried to distract herself from the reality of the situation by looking at the faces around them. If she thought too hard about the shiny wooden box in front of them, she would burst into tears.

In the first row sat Tammy, quiet as a stone and completely alone. Other strangers dotted the rows in front. Lou was two rows behind them, the look on his face like he was holding in a sneeze.

Trying to look sad, most likely.

Traitor. He'd broken Justine's heart. She'd fallen apart after that divorce. More than once, Justine had called Val in the middle of the night, all desperation and sobs.

"Should I call him?" she would ask. "Beg him for another chance?"

Val always gave her a confident, resolute, *no.* She promised Justine she'd soon move on to bigger and better things.

It seemed Justine didn't quite manage to do that in the years following the divorce, though. Val wasn't sure what she had been up to, exactly. Justine had just stopped calling about it, and it was honestly a bit of a relief. Val knew nothing about divorce. Not really.

What insight did she have? What comfort could she offer? All those nights when she dashed to answer Justine's calls, she'd left her husband snoozing peacefully in their bed.

Though they'd had their fair share of blowouts over the years, she was comfortable in the fact that they'd done things right. They'd waited to get married until they were older, until they knew what they wanted, and they were incredibly well-matched.

It wasn't until this year, on the eve of their twentieth anniversary party, that her own traitor of a husband showed his true colors and told her, "I'm sorry. I'm not in love with you anymore."

He wouldn't be allowed at her funeral – if he outlived her. Val smiled to herself. He didn't have a chance, not with his high cholesterol and inability to remember to take his medications.

"Thank you all for coming here today to honor the life of our dear friend, Justine Emerald."

Val sucked in a shaky breath. It was incomprehensible that Justine was gone. She half expected her to jump out and tell them it was all a prank.

She never did, though, and the service pressed on. Some stranger got up and shared a memory of the first time they met Justine. Then another stranger read a poem – *Death is Nothing at All.*

Val liked that one. They'd read it at her neighbor's funeral. The guy had just dropped dead one day when he was watering his flowers. Not a bad way to go.

She looked down at her nails, studying the chipped paint on her pointer finger. She needed something to look at in order not to cry. No one else was crying, and she wasn't going to be the one to start.

That was an honor reserved for Tammy, not Val. Really, the person who seemed to be having the hardest time keeping it together was Zora.

Poor Zora. Lost a friend *and* she was out of a job.

Music started playing again, and people were getting up. Val was surprised. The service felt short.

"Was that it?" she asked.

"I think so." Michelle shrugged. "She must've had a bigger service back home."

Lisa shook her head. "No. This is the only one. Zora told me – she planned the whole thing."

"Event planning must not be her strong suit," Val said, eyeing the barren refreshments table.

The overpowering smell of stale cigarette smoke filled her nostrils. Val knew who it was before she turned around.

Tammy.

"I was glad to see you three here."

"Mrs. Miller, I'm so sorry for your loss. We're all devastated," Michelle said.

Tammy nodded. Her blue eyes were so clouded that it was hard to tell who she was looking at. It made Val uneasy.

"You girls want to stop by for a cup of tea?"

Before Val could think of an excuse, Lisa said, "Of course. We'd love to!"

"I can give you a ride," she said, turning slowly and walking with her cane toward the mass of parked cars.

Val dropped her voice. "If we get into her car, I'd say there's a fifty percent chance one of us won't make it."

"And it won't be Tammy," Lisa added.

Michelle bit her lip before yelling out, "We'll meet you there, okay?"

Tammy responded with a grunt as she climbed into her car.

"We need to have an exit plan," Michelle said, dropping her voice. "The years have not been kind to Mrs. Miller. She spends a lot of time at county council meetings yelling at people and making demands."

"Demands about what?" asked Lisa.

"Last year she proposed a dress code for visitors to the island, punishable by a night in the county jail."

Lisa's face brightened. "Hey, that could be fun! I wonder if I'd pass?"

They were halfway to Michelle's car when Zora caught up to them. "Ladies! When would be a good time to talk to the three of you? Justine left some..." Her voice cracked. "Things to discuss."

Keep it together, Zora.

"Things?" asked Michelle.

Zora nodded.

Michelle shrugged and spoke again. "When were you thinking? We can meet at my café in Friday Harbor, as long as no one is in a rush?"

Val didn't have a ride home yet, so it made no difference to her.

Zora recovered from her near blubbering and smiled. "Yes, well, I'll be ready in about three hours?"

"Ah," Lisa made a face. "I was hoping to get back tonight. I left my car at the ferry terminal."

"You'll still be able to make the ferry," Michelle said.

"Oh, all right then." Lisa shrugged. "I trust you."

Zora was already being pulled away by a serious-faced man. "I'll see you then!"

They piled into Michelle's car and drove the familiar route to Justine's childhood home. The house hadn't changed much, but not in a good way. It looked like nothing had been updated in years. The siding was sagging and discolored from years in the sun. The grass was overgrown, as were the trees and shrubs in the front of the house.

The highlight of the entire little property was a handful of lavender bushes that would've been taller than Val were she not wearing four-inch heels.

"Come in. Hurry up, you're letting all the bugs in," Tammy said, waving a hand from the front door.

Val forced a smile as they stepped inside. Somehow the house seemed even smaller than she remembered it, and she'd never thought it was all that big.

"What kind of tea do you want?" Tammy asked, thumping toward the kitchen with her cane.

"What kind do you have?" asked Lisa, walking ahead.

"Lipton."

Lisa maintained her airy, upbeat tone. "Lipton would be great."

They sat at the kitchen table, and though it was different than the one from their childhood, Val still somehow felt like she was a little girl again, in trouble for putting firecrackers where they didn't belong.

"Did you see him there? I can't believe the nerve." Tammy slammed a teakettle onto the stove.

"Who, exactly?" asked Val.

"The distinguished Mr. Louis Emerald, of course,"

Val had the impression that if Tammy weren't in her own kitchen, she would've spat.

"I wasn't sure he'd come," Michelle said.

"If he had any decency, he wouldn't have." She lit a cigarette, the flame smoldering in her eyes. "Brought that teenager with him. Disgusting."

The woman had a point. Val made a grunt of agreement.

"Don't think on it," Lisa said. "I wouldn't."

"Don't think on it? That man killed my daughter."

Val looked down at her hands. She was never quite as good at handling Tammy as Lisa was. It seemed she still didn't have that skill, even decades later.

"I know you're grieving, but – "

Tammy cut her off. "Of course I'm grieving, but I'm not stupid. Justine was healthy. She was young. How can a daughter die before her mother? What kind of tragedy is that? Do you know what kind of nightmare that is?"

Lisa pinched her lips together. "I can't imagine."

"He took out an insurance policy on her when they were married. Did you know that?"

Michelle, using her best calming voice, said, "I'm sure that was sorted in the divorce."

The teakettle started a quiet whistle, and Val jumped to tend to it. The sooner they drank the tea, the sooner they could get out of here.

Tammy paid her no attention. "They cremated her before I even knew she was dead. Can you imagine?"

Val frowned. Sounded like something her own soon-to-be ex-husband would do. All he cared about now was his twenty-two-year-old girlfriend. Twenty-two! She was less than half his age!

"How have you been doing, Mrs. Miller?" asked Lisa, reaching out to grab her hand. "Have you been keeping busy?"

Tammy shrugged her off. "I'm always busy. Justine was busy, too. She could never visit, like the rest of you. Now we have all manner of freaks moving to the island, blasting their music and – "

Val plopped the teas onto the table. "Where's the sugar, Mrs. Miller?"

She paused, staring in Val's general direction. "What do you need sugar for? You're not little girls anymore. You can't be wasting sugar to put into tea. Does everything have to be sweet?"

"You're right. This is delicious just as it is." Val blew on her cup, taking as big a chug as she could and burning the entirety of her tongue.

Michelle managed to successfully steer the conversation to current events on the island. Tammy had complaints about each of them, but she seemed less disgruntled in general.

They finished their tea in record time and made excuses to leave. Tammy didn't protest.

Once they were back in the car, Michelle confronted Valerie. "Thanks for hardly saying anything in there."

"Yeah, Val. Nice work," Lisa added.

Val crossed her arms. "I tried to get you some sugar. That was my last stand."

"Sugar's last stand," Lisa mused, snorting a laugh.

"I feel bad for the lady," Val continued, "but I don't know how to handle her. You were both doing so well. Who am I to interfere?"

Lisa turned around and flashed a smile. "I forgot there are no old people in Los Angeles. You've lost your touch."

"Ha ha." Val rolled her eyes. "There are plenty of old people in LA. You just don't see them up in their mansions."

Lisa let out a gasp. "Michelle! Do you still make those little pies at the café? I've been dreaming about them all week."

Michelle nodded, eyes focused on the road. "We do. We can head over early, if you'd like?"

They all agreed, and off they went, gabbing and talking over one another. Such was the mysterious charm of old friends. It felt like they'd picked up right where they'd left off, and Val, at least, was thankful for it.

Four

They arrived at the café to find a line of people extending out to the sidewalk. Michelle wasn't surprised to see it, but her friends were.

Val let out a dramatic sigh and said, "Guess there's no room for us."

"They probably ate all of the mini pies, too," Lisa added.

Michelle pulled the car into her reserved parking spot. She didn't need Val getting into a spat with one of her customers, telling them to make way. "There are pies. Don't worry. We can go upstairs. I finally got around to remodeling it."

Michelle hoped the staff wasn't overwhelmed by all of the people. She normally would step in and help, but she had guests. Maybe she could still pop in...

"Oh la la! Fancy!" Val got out, pushing her sunglasses to the top of her head. "Your mom used to get so annoyed when we would sneak up there and dig through the old garbage. What'd you do with all of that stuff?"

"I threw most of it away," Michelle said, locking the car doors. "Some of it was useful to the historical society, though."

She opened the back door of the café and almost ran into Nelly, one of her employees. "Sorry! Is everything okay? Do you want me to jump in?"

Yoga Nelly, as they called her, responded with her customary cool. "It's all good. No worries. You going up?"

Michelle nodded. "If a woman named Zora comes looking for us, can you tell her where we are?"

Nelly flashed a smile and grabbed a to-go container. "Sure thing, boss."

Having good employees was the difference between life and death in the food industry. Michelle was thankful for her staff.

Well, except for Lola. Lola was terrible. She'd called in sick today. Again. There was always one. Hopefully she'd quit soon.

Michelle led the way up the stairs, and Lisa and Val followed.

"Shell, this is incredible!" Lisa said. "It looks like something out of a home magazine."

"Thanks." It'd been a lot of work, but she'd ended up with a lot more time on her hands after her son Tyler had gone off to school.

"What're you drinking? And eating? I can bring up whatever you'd like."

Val clapped her hands together. "Do you have cappuccinos?"

"Of course."

"I'll take one of those, please."

"I believe you owe me a doughnut," Lisa replied, tapping her chin, "but I'll accept a coffee and a small pie."

Michelle laughed. "Coming right up."

She popped back downstairs, made their drinks, and loaded a tray for the trip up the stairs. Her waitressing days served her well – nothing was out of balance, and she didn't lose a single drop on the trek up.

When she got back, Val and Lisa were still walking around and exclaiming how nice everything looked.

Val had her hand on a doorknob to the second room. "What's over there?"

"A little apartment. You can open the door. It's empty now."

"What do you do with it?"

"I rent it out. No one's here this week, though."

Val opened the door and she and Lisa walked in, followed by another three straight minutes of praise.

Michelle didn't stop them. She was proud of how things had turned out. It had taken her months to get this place into shape, and all of the design choices were bohemian and minimalistic, just as she liked it.

"It's completely marvelous," Lisa said, accepting her mini pie and taking a seat at the small table in the office. "Your mom would be so proud, Shell. Of everything."

"Thanks. We've had some lean years, but I've managed to keep things afloat."

"Did you ever find the time to go for those marine biology classes?" asked Lisa.

Michelle took a sip of her coffee. "No. The restaurant takes up most of my time."

"That's too bad." Val took a seat. "You'd think, with all the online schools now, it'd be easier."

As if it were ever easy. Michelle had to keep this old café running. Her mom had entrusted it to her. Her parents, both children of Trinidadian immigrants, had started with nothing. They'd put their everything into this place. Michelle had to keep it alive, regardless of whatever whimsical dreams she had for herself.

Besides, she'd never managed to save up much of a college fund for her son, let alone one for herself.

"Even online school is expensive," Michelle said with a sigh. "Tyler being in school is enough."

"What year is he now?" asked Lisa. "Don't tell me he's finished medical school and I missed it."

A smile spread across Michelle's face. "Not yet, but he's in his last year. He'll be matching to residency soon."

"What's he going into?" Val asked. "Please say plastic surgery. I'd love to have a personal connection to an expert."

"Don't be silly," Michelle said with a laugh. "He enjoyed his oncology rotation, so he's thinking he'll focus on that."

Lisa put a hand to her chest. "God bless him. He's always had a heart of gold. He gets that from you, Michelle."

Michelle couldn't help it; she was beaming. "No, not from me. He takes after his dad. I see so much of Ben in him."

"He was a great guy," Lisa said wistfully.

Michelle nodded. "The best."

It had been sixteen years since Ben had passed away. It all happened so suddenly – one minute he was there, her handsome, kind, gentle husband, smiling in the sun. The next minute, he'd collapsed, never to rise again.

A blood clot had killed him. A stupid blood clot. It was the first sign of a clotting disorder he'd never known about. He didn't get a second sign.

A few years later, Justine had a teeny, tiny, little stroke that warned her of a similar condition. Yet she got on a blood thinner and never had another problem with it.

Such was life. Though she missed him less often, she didn't miss him any less intensely. Love was strange like that.

"What about you?" asked Michelle. "How are Neil and the kids?"

"Wonderful!" Lisa took a bite of pie. "Avery just finished his master's degree and got a job in Portland. Sierra is still in Seattle, working her way up the corporate ladder."

"How's Neil been with, you know," Val dropped her voice, "his gambling?"

Lisa's eyes didn't leave her plate. She carefully picked the last crumbs of pie with her fork. "You know, he has his ups and downs. We take it one day at a time." She looked up, reaching for her coffee cup. "How's Reggie?"

Val rolled her eyes. "You know, fine, but we're going through different stages of our lives, and we've realized we grew apart."

"Oh no," Lisa said. "Can't you work it out?"

"I'm too wise to waste any more time on him," Val said matter-of-factly. "We're getting a divorce."

Michelle set down her teacup. "A divorce?"

"A divorce!" Lisa echoed, eyes wide.

"Yes, a divorce," Val said airily. "Don't make a big deal out of it. I don't know anybody who gets past twenty years anymore. The world just changes too much. Who wants to be with the same person?"

Michelle said nothing. She would've given anything to still have Ben.

"Speak for yourself," Lisa said. "Neil and I are going twenty-seven years strong."

"Wouldn't you like an upgrade?" Val asked with a wry smile.

Michelle couldn't help it—she let out a chortle of a laugh. If Lisa hadn't upgraded Neil by now, nothing was going to convince her.

"No." Lisa's eyes darted between them. "You don't just toss people away when they don't suit your needs anymore. That's not what I believe."

"Oh, don't get all sanctimonious on me," Val said. "It's not about *my* needs. We just don't make each other happy. Who wants to suffer through that?"

"True," Lisa relented. "But everything can't always be sunshine and rainbows."

Michelle bit her lip. Lisa was clearly offended, and Val obviously hadn't noticed. She needed to intervene. "Well, you have kids," Michelle offered. "I think that makes the equation a bit more complicated."

"Oh please!" Val tossed her head back. "I don't need to have kids to know when it's time to call it quits. There's a ninety-nine percent chance that you and Ben would've been divorced by now if he were still alive."

Michelle felt the anger rush through her chest. She managed to stop herself and think before she reacted, though. Apparently all that yoga her friends had dragged her to was good for something.

After a moment, she responded. "I don't think so."

A knock carried through the door and they startled like a trio of barn owls.

"Who's that?" Lisa whispered.

Michelle shrugged and called out, "Come in!"

She hoped it was Zora with impeccable timing, but it ended up being someone much worse.

Arthur.

Michelle's heart sank.

"Hey! I'm sorry. I didn't know you had company."

Val stood, extending a hand. "I don't think we've met before. I'm Valerie Villano. I'm sure Michelle talks about me all the time."

A polite smile crossed Arthur's face and he accepted Val's handshake. "Yes, of course. Val, it's nice to finally meet you."

"And I'm Lisa." She didn't get up, instead waving from her seat.

"I was so sorry to hear about your friend Justine," he said. "It sounds like you were all so close."

Michelle shifted in her chair. So he *did* listen when she told him things. Perhaps he wasn't even pretending to remember who Val and Lisa were.

"I don't mean to interrupt," he said, turning toward the door. "I just wanted to see how you're doing, Michelle."

She forced a smile. "Fine. We're all good, actually. Just catching up."

"If you need me to help out here, or cover the café for you for a couple of days, it's no problem. Take whatever time you need."

Actually, this dress was the wrong material for summer. Maybe this decade. Did it have wool in it? It was too hot. Michelle could feel heat creeping up her entire body. "Thanks, Arthur. I appreciate it, but I'm okay."

He nodded, then ducked out of the room.

They started on her immediately.

"Excuse me. Why didn't you tell us about handsome Arthur?" Val asked, hands on her hips.

"There's nothing to tell. He owns the bakery two doors down and sometimes we...collaborate."

Lisa winked at her. "Collaborate, eh?"

"He's a *business* associate," Michelle said firmly. "You two vultures can calm down."

"Vultures!" Val exclaimed, a look of mock horror on her face. "We're your friends, Michelle. Your oldest friends."

"That's right," Lisa said solemnly. "You know you're allowed to date, right? We won't tell your mom."

Michelle stood, picking up their empty plates and cups and loading them onto the tray. "Have you been dating, Val?"

"I wish I had the time!" Val let out a sigh, dropping back into her seat. "I'm trying to get a new album recorded. Plus I need to plan a tour, PR, and everything while dealing with the divorce. Reggie was a crap manager, you know. There's so much for me to clean up."

"Ah, I see." Michelle finished cleaning as Val elaborated on the plans she had for her singing career.

She'd always been talented, and at one point, she was even successful. For a moment, it seemed like their little small town friend Val would be a worldwide sensation.

But for whatever reason, the moment had passed and left Val behind. She had never given up the fight, though.

Michelle waited for a break in the story to excuse herself. She needed to carry the tray downstairs and check on Nelly.

● ● ●

Mercifully, when Michelle returned, the conversation had changed to memories of Justine. Zora arrived to find a much happier bunch.

"I know you're all busy, so I'll cut to the chase," she said, taking a seat.

Michelle sat back. That seemed like an alarming statement, though neither Lisa nor Valerie reacted.

"As I told Lisa, I'm the executor of Justine's estate. I've been busy trying to get things in order, and I'm sorry I haven't been able to reach out to you yet."

"Did Justine leave us something?" asked Val.

"Yes. Sort of." Zora reached into her bag and pulled out a gold folder marked Girls' Trip.

Michelle stared at it. It was clearly Justine's swoopy handwriting in elaborate, glittery ink. What adult woman kept glitter markers? Only Justine could pull it off.

"Justine immensely valued the friendship you shared. She talked about you all the time."

Tears rushed to Michelle's eyes and she swallowed, commanding them to retreat.

"She would go on about how hard it was to get everyone together, and a few years ago, she got the idea of hosting a girls' trip." Zora opened the folder, pulling out a stack of pictures and a paper labeled Itinerary.

"The problem was, the trip she'd planned centered around the properties she shared with Lou. When he filed for divorce, she lost access to the properties in Miami and Santa

Monica, though she got to keep the one in Bar Harbor. She struggled with how to make this trip work without them, and put off re-planning it until recently."

Michelle frowned. Why had Justine never told them about this? They could've stayed at a Howard Johnson for all she cared.

Zora went on. "Before she died, Justine was working on a new plan that went to the same cities so she could show you all of her favorite restaurants and spots. She wanted to show you the best of everything, and she was saving up for the trip."

Saving? Surely Justine had gotten a significant settlement in the divorce? The guy was a grifter, sure, but he was a rich grifter.

Not long after Justine and Lou had met, they started a company called Emerald Life. It was, in essence, a self-help company, but it grew into something much larger. Within a decade, Emerald Life had thousands of members and was pulling in millions a year. Michelle had read an article about it in Vanity Fair. It was not entirely flattering, with accusations that the organization functioned like a cult in some ways.

None of that was Justine's doing, though. Lou had taken more and more control of the business until Justine had no say at all.

"I'm going to cry," Lisa said, shaking her head and picking up a box of tissues from the corner. After returning to her seat, she offered the box around.

"I know this is a lot to handle," Zora said, accepting a tissue and blowing her nose. "Justine was in the process of planning the trip when she died, and she actually included a request in her will."

"A request?" Val leaned forward.

Zora nodded. "A request. I have it here. Hang on a second." She fumbled through some papers before pulling out a sheet and clearing her throat. "Dear friends, if you are reading this, I am back on my home planet."

Michelle snickered. *Typical Justine.*

"Just kidding." Zora smiled and took a deep breath before continuing. "I'm dead, apparently. I hope I went out in a really cool way, like saving kittens from a fire, but if not, please make up an appropriate story.

"I'm still hoping you'll never see this letter and I'll find the time to go on this trip with you myself. But if you're hearing this, then I messed up. I've left instructions with Zora to plan the most epic girls' trip that ever was.

"Actually, I guess we don't so much find time as we make time. We've been friends for so long that it's easy to take one another for granted. Easy to take our connection for granted. If I let myself use being busy as an excuse, then shame on me. Don't follow in my footsteps (unless it's the saving kittens thing. Then you probably should).

"Please, make the time to be together. Our friendship deserves it. You deserve to have the time of your lives. I will come along, in ash and in spirit. Sprinkle my remains as you wish. I believe ashes can be used as a weapon in close combat situations, too, so don't forget that. Please remember – "

Zora reached for a tissue, a sob caught in her throat. "I'm sorry," she said, blowing her nose. She cleared her throat and returned to reading. "Please remember no one has ever known me like you three, and no one could ever love me like you did. Love you always, Justine."

Val was the first to sob, and a moment later, there wasn't a dry eye in the room.

Except for Michelle, who sat with her arms firmly crossed and her lips pinched shut. She was not going to cry in front of everyone. She was not going to break down, no matter how awful this situation was.

Since she was the only one capable of speech, she spoke first. "That was very sweet of her. It's too bad we can't all pack up and go on a trip, though."

Val's mouth popped open. "What? Didn't you hear what she said? We need to *make* the time."

Michelle stared at her. She couldn't be serious.

"I'm in," Lisa said shakily. "I don't even care where we're going, I'll do whatever Justine wanted."

No. This wasn't happening. This was completely impractical. "Lisa, I mean – don't you have to go to work?"

She waved a hand and dabbed at her eyes. "I'm actually between jobs right now. It's perfect timing."

"Me too," Val said, nodding. "Justine's right. What if you're the next to go, Michelle? What if we never get to take Justine on her last trip?"

Lisa let out a sob. "Her last trip."

This was ridiculous. "I'm sorry, but I can't do it," she said, standing and tidying the table. "I have a business here, and a life. It's the busy season and – "

Val cut her off. "Oh, come on. That hunky baker can take care of the café for you. He said he doesn't mind."

"It's not that easy," Michelle said. "There's inventory, and I have to make sure our orders get here from the mainland, and my employees have to – "

"He'll figure it out," Lisa said confidently. "Zora, did you already plan everything?"

Zora nodded. "Yes, almost entirely. First, you'll go to Miami beach, then to Santa Monica, and finally to Justine's house in Maine."

Michelle rubbed her face with her hands. How could they even consider this? It was sweet, and of course they were all sad, but come on.

"What's that face?" Val asked. "Are these places not good enough for you?"

"Oh." Lisa dropped her voice. "Michelle's afraid of flying."

"Aw, still?" Val poked her in the shoulder. "That's so cute."

"That's not it." Michelle kept her tone steady and firm. "I can't go. I'm sorry, but that's final. You two can still have a nice time without me, and I wish you the best."

June 10th, 1990

Zora could tell her presence was no longer needed at the café. Valerie and Lisa were animated, gesticulating wildly, while Michelle stared them down with the expression of a brick wall. There was only one thing left to do.

None of them noticed when Zora reached into her bag and slipped a thin notebook into the Girls' Trip folder.

"My number is in here," she said, sliding the folder over. "Please give me a call to let me know what you decide."

She stood and walked away, a smile on her lips. The diary was bookmarked at Justine's entry from June 10th, 1990.

Dear diary,

I can't believe the Fabulous Four are graduating from high school! I never thought this day would come. I feel so old!

Shell, Val, and Lisa are all getting ready for college in the fall. I'm happy for them, and soon, I'll be able to join them. I've got a plan.

Mom says my plan is stupid, but now that I'm eighteen, she can't stop me. I'm moving to Seattle, getting a job, and saving money for school. By this time next year, I'll be getting my degree.

I already have a job lined up at a cute smoothie place in the city. Mom thinks I should stay here, but I think she's just worried because she never went to school and hardly ever leaves the island. She'll be proud of me in the end, I'm sure of it.

I'm excited, scared, and a little sad. It'll be hard for the Fabulous Four to be apart for a year. I'll try to visit everyone, and I'll keep reminding myself how lucky I am.

Any time I feel sad, I'll work on my gratitude journal. I am so, so grateful for my friends. I know we'll be friends forever, and a few years apart won't make a difference. I'm grateful I got to have three best friends for the last thirteen years. Most people don't even get one real friend.

I'm grateful for Valerie and her unstoppable spirit. I know she'll achieve everything she's ever wanted, and the University of Washington is getting an amazing musician.

I'm grateful for Lisa always being there for me. Every time I had a fight with Mom and needed somewhere to sleep, every time I needed a partner in crime, Lisa was there for me. Even when I said something thoughtless, Lisa and her big heart forgave me. I love her to pieces.

I think I might miss Michelle most of all. She got an amazing scholarship to Northeastern University, and I know she's going to save all the dolphins and the fish and the coral reefs like she's always dreamed. But before she saved the world, Michelle saved me, again and again. She's so wise, and smart, and the strongest person I know.

Look out world, the class of 1990 is coming for you!
- Justine

Five

The plane touched down and the pilot's buttery-smooth voice rolled over the speaker. "Hey folks, welcome to beautiful, sunny Miami. Today's high is ninety-three degrees, and there's a ten percent chance of rain. We wish you a pleasant stay in paradise and hope to see you again very soon. On behalf of all our crew, thank you for flying..."

The champagne had gone to Lisa's head. She turned her goofy, smiling face toward Michelle, who had only just pried her fingers off of the armrest.

"See? In first class, flying isn't so bad," Val said, downing the rest of the whiskey sour she'd hidden from the flight attendant.

"I just don't understand why we couldn't have gone to Santa Monica first, then Miami, and then Maine," Michelle said. "Why do we have to fly back and forth across the country so many times? The flights are so long, and our carbon footprint is – "

Lisa cut her off. "I'm sure Justine thought it was part of the fun. You know, spending more time in first class. I know I enjoyed it."

Lisa never thought she'd get to fly first class. She loved everything about it, from the hot towel when she got on board to the drinks to the little cheeses that came individually wrapped. She took a dozen pictures to show her kids.

Val popped up from her seat and fluffed her long, blonde hair. Somehow she always managed to keep it looking nice. "We get to get off first, too. The perks never end!"

Lisa agreed. First class was the way to live. If only she'd ever had money. It was just a small complication, really.

She giggled to herself before following Val off the plane in a giddy haze.

The Miami airport matched her mood, bursting with life and lights and sound. Beeping motorized carts flew by as people darted to their gates. There was a rowdy group drinking at a nearby bar, and there seemed to be some sort of breakdancing practice at an empty gate.

Heavenly smells drifted from the restaurants along the walkway. Lisa rolled her suitcase behind her, feeling like she was floating on a cloud. Would it be ridiculous for her to grab a snack before they left? There might not be anything close to the hotel.

"Does anyone want to split a pizza?" she asked.

Val shook her head. "I'm still full from the plane."

"You didn't eat anything!"

Val shrugged in response.

Lisa tried to catch up to Michelle to see if she'd agree to something, but she was too far ahead.

"Slow down! It's not a race!" Lisa called out.

Michelle stopped and turned around. "We don't want to miss our bags. I never should've checked mine. What if it didn't get on the plane?"

Val and Lisa exchanged looks, but before they could say anything, Michelle was off again, yelling over her shoulder. "Come on!"

"Ooh, you're in trouble," Val cooed.

"I already have my bag. I can't be rushed," Lisa said, head held high. "I haven't had a vacation in years. I'm going to go as slow as possible."

She and Val sauntered through the airport, giggling like school girls. They were debating the practicality of getting a massage in the middle of the airport while Michelle glared at them from afar.

She was not amused. "How much did you guys drink on the plane?"

"Not enough," Val said, taking a wobbly step onto the escalator.

Lisa followed, more stable since she wasn't wearing heels. "Oh look! That billboard has a killer whale on it. Do you want to go see the whale, Shell? We can add that to the itinerary for you."

"No!" Michelle let out a huff. "Absolutely not. I'm not going to support them keeping her captive in that tiny tank. Do you know it's only twenty feet deep, and she's twenty feet long!"

"Is that so?"

"The tank is only thirty-five feet wide. It's a crime."

"Don't tell me you know her?" Val said, a smile dancing on her lips. "The whale?"

"I do, and both of you should, too." Michelle stared at them, waiting for response. When none came, she pushed on. "That's Lolita. Her Salish name is Tokitae. Does that ring a bell?"

"You're on a first name basis with this whale?" Val put her hands up. "I'm sorry if I've offended your relationship."

Finally, Michelle let out a laugh. "I'm not offended; I just thought you'd remember. Lolita is a Southern Resident orca. She's one of *us*. Her family still comes to San Juan every summer."

"Wait, I do remember you telling us this," Lisa said. They'd reached baggage claim, and she was relieved to see that their carousel had not started moving yet. Michelle might've lost it if she spotted her bag brazenly enjoying rides around the airport without her.

"Yes, they drowned four baby whales during the capture." Michelle let out a sigh. "Sixteen members of the pod were either taken or killed back then. The pod never recovered – they're still endangered to this day."

"You don't need a marine biology degree," Val said. "You already know everything."

"Hardly," Michelle said, but a smile had crept onto her face. "Lolita's mom is still alive. She swims with her pod around the islands."

"That's actually really sad." Lisa frowned. "I wish we could reunite them."

"I agree." Michelle crossed her arms, shifting her weight. "I will not give a dollar to the place that's kept her trapped for the last fifty-two years."

The whale had been in that tiny tank for fifty-two years? That was longer than Lisa had been alive.

That put it in perspective. What a nightmare. And she thought her marriage felt never-ending.

Val pulled a piece of paper from her pocket. "I don't think freeing a whale is on our itinerary for today, but I'm not against discussing it."

"Don't tease me," Michelle said. "I'm just...you know."

Val reached forward and squeezed her shoulder. "I know. You care. I've always liked that about you."

She rolled her eyes. "Thanks, Val."

Bags started to appear, and Michelle's focus changed to securing a good view of the belt. People were now crowding and rushing forward, making it difficult to see.

Michelle's mood darkened accordingly. "Okay, no need to stand in front of me," she said under her breath, elbowing out the young couple who had overtaken her spot.

It was hard not to laugh. Lisa debated whether she should get out of the way or report to Michelle's side as backup. The decision was made for her when someone pushed her from behind.

"First class isn't helping us here," Lisa said, shaking her head. "We're going to get trampled if our bags don't show up soon."

"How is it that there are so many people and no one is taking any of these bags?" Michelle asked, the volume of her voice increasing. "Did they send the wrong bags to the wrong place? What does that tag say? Can you see, Lisa?"

She squinted. "It says MIA. Is that Miami, or missing in action?"

"We're in the right place," Val said soothingly. "Relax. If anyone pushes you, step on them. Listen, I've got something to add to the itinerary."

"This better not be another joke about Lolita," Michelle said firmly.

"Yeah," Lisa added. "It's not funny, Val."

"No, it's not about that." Val dropped her voice. "I think we should look into Tammy's theory."

Lisa tapped her chin and let out a long "Hm." All that alcohol made her think she was funny. It was an unusual feeling for her. "Do you mean about how too much riffraff is moving to the island?"

"Or that loud music and bare midriffs will be the downfall of society?" suggested Michelle, reaching forward and pulling her bag off the belt.

Val waved a hand. "No, none of that. I mean about Lou killing Justine."

Lisa eyed her warily. She couldn't always tell when Val was kidding.

Michelle's eyes were still on the belt, diligently scanning for Val's bags. "Don't tell me you believe her. What motive would he have?"

"Not having to pay alimony anymore? Dark secrets she was going to reveal?" Val pulled her phone out. "Who knows? As someone involved in a bitter divorce, I'm sure it's crossed Reggie's mind to kill me off."

Lisa shushed her. "Someone's going to hear you and you'll be checked into an asylum before I can even get my first piña colada."

Val leaned in, pointing to a picture on her phone. "I found a way to get into Justine's old beach house."

"No. Stop," Michelle said, eyes closed. "We're not breaking into Lou's beach house."

"We don't have to break in. I found a job posting for it."

Lisa grabbed the phone out of her hand. Sure enough, there was a bright red "accepted" on the screen. "A maid job?" she asked. "Will I have to wear one of those little outfits?"

Val shook her head. "It's not like that. It's an actual cleaning job. This app, Skillz – I use it sometimes back home – lets you find someone to drop in and clean on short notice."

Michelle looked skeptical. "Is that like Uber for house cleaning?"

"Yeah, exactly! There are other jobs, too, like mowing grass, pool cleaning, tutoring – I mean, you get the idea. It's the perfect opportunity to look around."

"No, it isn't," Michelle said, reaching forward and heaving Val's smaller bag from the belt. "If Lou sees us walk in there, he's going to call the police. He's not stupid."

Lisa made a face. "Well, I don't know about that. He's kind of stupid."

"He's not home," Val said. "Look, he's posting pictures of himself right now. He's in the Maldives on a spiritual retreat."

Lisa let out a groan. The water was blue and crystal clear. "Can we clean his house there instead?"

"I thought this was a spa trip," Michelle said, dragging the second bag off of the belt and dropping it with a grunt. "I wasn't planning on doing manual labor."

"Suit yourself." Val shrugged. "I'll go on my own."

That giddy feeling crept over Lisa again. "I'm going with you, Val!"

"Guys!" Michelle looked exasperated. "I thought we were doing what Justine wanted us to do. Getting our nails done and bonding or whatever."

"There's plenty of time for that," Val said. "What kind of friends would we be if we didn't even look into her death?"

Lisa had nothing to add. Tammy was kooky and angry, but what if she had a point? What harm was it to entertain the idea?

Michelle said nothing as the car rental shuttle pulled up. "Don't forget your other suitcase," she barked, stepping on board.

Six

The cat was out of the bag. Now they understood why Val had insisted on renting a car at the airport instead of being picked up by a limousine as Justine had suggested.

Val had come up with her house-snooping plan right after Michelle had broken down and agreed to the trip. She'd stayed up most of the night, powered by her new obsession with Lou, and frantically tried to find a way to get inside the house. She didn't question where the energy was coming from. She didn't need to. She was onto something real.

At first, Val had dismissed Tammy's ramblings about Lou murdering Justine. Nothing else Tammy said made sense, and it was too horrible for words.

Yet, no matter what she did, she couldn't get it out of her head. Lou was a scumbag—that was nothing new. But a murderer? The thought made the hair stand up on the back of her neck. He was, in some ways, a simple man, fueled by greed and ego.

Those were the type of men who killed, weren't they? If Justine had embarrassed him, or threatened his precious money, how would he have reacted? The divorce had taken years, and though Justine didn't talk of it much, Lou had raged against her every step of the way. What if he didn't get what he wanted? He probably wanted everything, which of course, was impossible. Even for generous Justine.

What if he'd come up with his own solution?

After Val had found the location of Lou's Miami house, the rest of her scheme fell into place. She'd changed her location in the Skillz app to Miami, just for kicks. Normally she tried to get jobs like singing lessons or celebrity drop-ins. Those happened often enough in LA.

Her friends didn't need to know she *occasionally* agreed to clean houses, too. The money was helpful, especially since sales of her old albums had disappeared over the last ten years or so, and it had been a few months since she'd done any performances. Reggie had never been a good manager; the divorce only made him more negligent.

Val didn't mind the cleaning jobs. It was fun to go inside those huge mansions, and she'd be back on her feet in no time.

"Won't it be a bit suspicious when we show up to clean in a ruby red convertible?" Michelle yelled from the backseat.

"They won't be home," Val said confidently. At least she hoped not. If only she'd thought to bring disguises.

"I love this," Lisa said clapping her hands together. "I haven't done anything this exhilarating in years."

"You mean this illegal?" Michelle asked. "You're right. My petty crime days ended after high school."

"You were always so good at keeping your cool, though," Val said. "We *need* you."

Michelle scoffed. "Looking at the itinerary, we have to check in to the Hotel Lusso, get our welcome drinks, and then have a five-course lunch by the pool. Nowhere in there do I see time to break in and clean Lou's house."

"We're not actually going to clean it," Val said as she aggressively cut onto the highway. If they were going to make it for the job, they needed to hurry up. "We'll go in, take a peek, and leave. We'll be back in time for lunch."

Hopefully.

"I'll be waiting for you by the pool," Michelle said.

Val kept quiet. Michelle had always refused to participate in her schemes until the very last minute. Then she'd give in as though she'd never protested at all.

It was possible Michelle had drastically changed over the years, but that seemed unlikely. People rarely changed. It wasn't that they *couldn't* change, but it took time, self-reflection, and effort. Most people settled for unfulfilled promises and bitterness.

Surely Michelle had other things to worry about than her one tiny personality flaw that occasionally got her into trouble.

They got to the hotel and their progress was slowed by Michelle and Lisa admiring the extravagance.

Val wasn't terribly impressed. It was nice, of course, but years ago, when her second album had come out and she went on a six-month tour, she stayed in what seemed like every five-star hotel in the country.

The novelty quickly wore off. There was no amount of hot stone aroma massages, shining white marble floors, or cascading infinity pools that made a hotel feel better than home.

"Let's drop our bags off, check out the room, and get down to the corner shop," she said, trying to rush them forward.

Lisa let out a groan. "I wanted to see the pool."

"There are multiple pools," Michelle said, pointing to the map in her hand. "There are also two spas, a fitness club, yoga on the beach...."

"Plenty of time for that later," Val said, calling the elevator. "After we get our cleaning supplies in order."

Lisa pulled her suitcase along, a smile permanently on her face. "Sure, sure."

Michelle followed behind, silent.

They got to the top floor, the penthouse, and the door clicked open to reveal a breathtaking view of the ocean.

"Are we really allowed to be in here?" Lisa asked in a low voice.

Val's bags had already arrived via the bellhop and she kicked them out of way so they could explore. A bottle of champagne and a box of chocolate-covered strawberries welcomed them. The three-bedroom suite was complete with a kitchen, an outdoor grill, a private hot tub, and an eighty-five-inch TV. There was a spiral staircase to the second floor, and Val could see a bed with crisp white linens and red rose petals to her right.

She opened the door to the balcony and stepped out. Even Val had to admit it was likely the most decadent and magnificent room in Miami Beach. They had a full view of the clear, turquoise ocean and the white sand beach below. A hammock swung lazily in the breeze next to their private, vibrantly blue plunge pool. The pool extended to the edge of the balcony, with a clear glass bottom that allowed a terrifying, yet entirely safe, view all the way down.

Michelle was stunned, still clutching her bag, which she'd refused to relinquish to the bellhop. "What do you think this cost Justine?"

"Probably twenty thousand dollars," Val replied, eyes fixed on the horizon. She managed to keep the glibness in her voice, though the thought of it made her sick. It was lot of money. Too much money, money Lou didn't want Justine to have.

But Justine didn't need it anymore, because Lou had killed her.

It didn't matter how crazy Michelle, or anyone, thought she was. Val knew she was right. She'd always been a big idea kind of person. She could see things others didn't. It was why she'd pursued a career as a singer. She knew she could do it. People thought she was crazy until her second album sold enough copies to get silver certification. She was only a few thousand short of gold.

It was true that Tammy's words had set her off. Even before that, though, she couldn't have been the only one to think that Justine's out-of-the-blue death was odd. *Justine*, who had started a company all about wellness, both of mind and body, had just up and died? No one thought that was suspicious? She was supposed to outlive them all.

Except. Except, except, except. She'd started her business with a power fiend. Lou Emerald. That was her only mistake – loving the wrong man.

It happened to the best of them.

"Look!" Lisa shouted. "My name is written on this cookie!" Val shot her a look. The cookie was the size of a dinner plate.

"It's good, too," Lisa said, mouth full.

Enough dilly dallying. Val unzipped her smaller bag and dumped a pile of clothing onto the floor. "I brought cleaning clothes for anyone who might need them. Old t-shirts and things."

"How long have you been planning this?" asked Michelle. There was a touch of astonishment and wonder to her voice.

"It all just sort of came together." Val ripped off her cute, beach-ready tank top with the seashells on the bust and threw on a raggedy t-shirt. "Don't be shy."

"Give me something," Lisa said, holding out a hand. "I'm not getting dressed in front of you, though."

Val handed her a yellow shirt. "We're going to see you in your swimsuit later."

"That's different," Lisa said brightly as she walked into a bedroom and shut the door.

"Is this why your bag was so heavy?" Michelle stood there, arms crossed. "You're going to get arrested."

"How can we be arrested if we're there to clean?" Val asked. "Seriously. Think about it."

She let out a sigh. "I guess I'll be the lookout."

Val beamed. "There's my girl! Take a shirt just in case. We've gotta go!"

● ● ●

Val made a call to the valet and, by the time they got downstairs, the car was waiting for them. She got them to the store in record time, threw together a bucket of cleaning supplies, and hopped back on the road.

Lou's house wasn't even on the beach. The six-thousand-square-foot home was located in the gated community of Star Island. It was a quick two-and-a-half-mile drive from their beachfront hotel, though of course, as often with the obscenely rich, the short drive felt like entering another world.

For thirty million, it came with a sparkling saltwater pool, nine bedrooms, ten bathrooms, and a dock deep enough for a "medium" yacht, whatever that meant.

They arrived at the neighborhood entrance and Val flashed her best Hollywood smile at the guard. "Melanie Tenderhook," she said confidently.

He looked at his clipboard, nodded, and pressed a button. The gate opened and off they went.

"Melanie *Tenderhook?*" Lisa snorted, causing even Michelle to laugh.

"Like I'm going to use my real name!" Val rolled her eyes. Miss Tenderhook happened to have a 4.7-star rating on Skillz, which was how they'd gotten approved for this job in the first place.

They drove down the palm tree-lined street as Michelle and Lisa gawked, trying to catch glimpses of the mansions behind the tall fences.

Val had her eyes on the prize. The white Spanish-style villa was just around the bend. She pulled up to the front gate, punched in the code she'd gotten from her temporary boss at Skillz, and on they drove.

The trees obscured most of the house from the street, but as they got closer, they got the full view. It looked even more gaudy in person.

Val could feel her jaw tighten. Justine never would've wanted this place. This house was all Lou.

She parked next to a fountain launching water twenty feet into the air.

Lisa took off her sunglasses, stumbling as she got out of the car. "How do we get in?"

"Follow me." Val led her to the door and rang the doorbell.

They waited. Then waited some more.

Maybe the doorbell wasn't hooked up? She rang it again, this time hearing the soft, delicate song echoing inside.

"The current housekeeper is the one that hired us," Val said in a whisper. "She must be busy. I can try to message her."

They waited so long that Michelle abandoned her lookout post in the car. "Okay, this was a nice idea, but it's clearly not working. It's time for us to go."

"No, no!" Val took her sunglasses off so she could better see her screen. "I'm just waiting to hear back from Debbie – "

The twelve-foot-tall door swung open to reveal a red-faced lady. "You're late! Get in here *now*!"

Debbie was so frightening that even Michelle obeyed her. Once they were inside, she shut the door and locked it. "I had three of my girls scheduled to clean this place, and all three of them called in sick. You know what makes me sick?" No one responded, so she answered herself. "*Them*."

She stomped off, dragging a large vacuum behind her. "Each one of you needs to do three bathrooms and three bedrooms in the next forty-five minutes. Do you hear me? Sparkling clean. Vacuum, sanitize, make the beds."

Val nodded. "Yes, sir."

Debbie stopped. "Do you think you're funny?" She leaned in and took a sniff. "Have you been drinking?"

Val vigorously shook her head. "Of course not. We're ready to work."

"Good. Get moving!"

Val handed them each a pair of gloves. "Here, Lisa, take the toilet bowl cleaner. Michelle, you can have the bleach wipes. There must be more supplies in the bathrooms. Dig around."

"I am not cleaning Lou's house," Michelle said, arms crossed.

"Just dust over some stuff and look in the closets and bedside tables for secrets."

Lisa's eyes grew wide. "How do we find the secrets?"

The woman popped her head back into the foyer. "I said get to work!"

"Going now!" Val said brightly, a wide smile on her face.

She was determined to find something, anything, that would prove her theory about Lou. She sprinted up the stupid, magnificent staircase, popping her head into each room until she found what seemed to be the master bedroom.

Despite rifling through all the nooks and drawers, she found nothing but some black T-shirts and a bottle of finasteride. Val Googled the doctor on the bottle. He was Miami's leading hair transplant specialist.

Heh.

She tidied up the bedroom and went into the bathroom. She gave the toilet, shower, and tub a light spray and wipe. It didn't look dirty. Why had they even been hired?

Her new boss came to check on her just as she was wiping the sinks. Val scrubbed with extra vigor.

"Not bad," Debbie said. "But work faster."

Val nodded, and once Scary Debbie was out of sight, she moved onto the next bedroom, and the next one, and the next one. There was so much furniture, and so many places to hide things, but it was all empty. This house had hardly been lived in at all.

She did another bathroom – one that actually had been used a few times – before finding an office.

Bingo. This was what she needed.

She tugged at the desk drawers, trying to force them to open. Where would Lou keep the key? In a cup, under the desk, hidden in a book? She couldn't find anything.

She was just about to pry into a drawer with a letter opener when she heard raised voices.

Val froze. It sounded like Michelle. She stopped what she was doing and strained to listen.

"Do *not* touch me."

Yep, that was definitely Michelle.

Val ran down the stairs as the voices grew louder.

"Opening packages? Are you insane? What are you, a thief? I'll call the police and – "

"It was already open," Michelle yelled back, never one to be outdone. "I was tidying up! The box needs to be thrown away."

As much as she loved seeing Michelle in her full form, fierce and immovable, this was going south quickly. "Ladies, ladies. What's the problem?"

Before anyone could answer, the front door opened. Val's heart dropped into her stomach like an anchor.

Seven

Michelle turned and froze. She recognized the woman who'd just walked into the house from the memorial. It was Lou's young-looking girlfriend.

"Oh, hi." She flashed an awkward smile and waved. "Don't mind me. I got in a bit early."

"I'm very sorry, Miss Chloe," Debbie said. "We were just finishing up. I am so sorry for the noise."

Chloe wheeled her little bag closer and shook her head. "It's not a problem, Debbie, not at all. I wanted to surprise Lou. I'll stay out of your way."

As Chloe walked past, Debbie nodded and tried to pry the package from Michelle's hands.

Michelle tightened her grip.

"We're done. We'll be going now." Debbie made a swift tug at the box, ripping the cardboard as she lost her grasp.

The sound of tearing made Chloe stop. "What's that?"

"Nothing, nothing." Debbie waved a hand, trying to usher Chloe out of the room. "It's a package for Mr. Emerald. It arrived damaged. I will place it in his office."

Chloe reached out a hand. "I can take it."

"No, I don't mind," Debbie said, trying to intercept the handoff.

Michelle wasn't going to miss her chance. She eluded Debbie's frantic reach and floated the box toward Chloe, open-side down. The canvas inside came crashing to the floor.

"Oh, sorry," Michelle said.

"It's okay!" Chloe was already squatting down, turning the painting over in her hands. "Thank you, I'll just put this..."

Michelle could feel Debbie's eyes boring into her, but she didn't care. She was focused on Lou's girlfriend.

Chloe hadn't gotten up from the floor. She was staring at the painting in her hands. Her eyes drifted up and down, finally settling onto the faces smiling back at her.

It was an oil painting of Lou with a brown-haired woman and a brown-haired little boy. A paper attached to the canvas said, "We love you, Daddy!"

Chloe finally broke her silence. "What is this?"

"Oh, who knows? I can take it upstairs," Debbie said. Her eyes bulged out of her head, a stark contrast to her still smile.

She reached for the canvas, but Chloe held onto it and looked up at all of them, eyes round. "I don't understand."

Ah. Michelle had been right. This was a secret family. She cleared her throat. "You didn't know? About Lou?"

Chloe stood and squared off with Michelle. "You know Lou?"

"All of you, out!" Debbie commanded, pointing a finger to the door.

Michelle ignored her. "Yes. I've known him for years."

"If I have to tell you one more time – "

"Pipe down, Debra," Val said. "You can leave if you want to."

Her nostrils flared. "You should not be touching that!"

Chloe turned to her. "Thank you, Debbie. I think we're all set for today."

Debbie shot one last glare at the three of them before taking her vacuum cleaner and stomping out.

Chloe turned to Michelle. "Did you bring this here?"

Michelle shook her head. "No. It was by the door. The box was damaged and...I looked inside."

Val's phone went off, merrily playing the chorus of her most popular song *I Won't Be Bringing Home the Bacon Anymore*.

She flashed a smile and answered it in a hushed voice. "Uh huh. Yes. Of course, we'll be right there. Give us ten minutes."

Lisa clapped her hands together. "Was that *our next job?* Gosh, we don't want to be late."

"No, it was Hotel Lusso." Val took her gloves off with a snap and patted Chloe on the shoulder. "Tough luck, love. Keep your chin up."

She pulled the front door open and disappeared into the blinding Miami sun. Lisa followed, and Michelle scooted past without making eye contact.

Eight

Back in the car, Val hit the gas and peeled out so wildly that she almost clipped the driveway gate.

Michelle's heart rate was through the roof. "I can't believe we just did that."

"You're a star!" Val yelled, turning around to flash a smile. "I told you we needed you."

Typical Val. Michelle didn't want to melt into her flattery, but it wasn't easy. She hadn't expected to find anything, particularly when she wasn't looking.

She really hadn't expected it to feel so *good*.

"Do you think we're going to get in trouble?" Lisa asked, fidgeting with her hands. Her face was fixed in such a severe frown it was almost comical.

Val turned to look at her. "Get in trouble for what? That house is spotless."

"You didn't make it very convincing that we were really there to clean!" Lisa's voice was high-pitched, bordering on a whine.

Michelle watched the houses go by. "I think the only one in trouble is Lou with his secret family."

Val slowed the car as they approached the community gate. "Yeah, that girl doesn't care about us."

The gate lifted automatically, releasing them.

"Oh good." Lisa clapped a hand to her chest. "I was afraid she would call security to have us stopped at the gate."

"What? Why?"

Lisa threw her hands up in the air. "Because she's clearly upset! Instead of blaming Lou, whom she should blame, she's probably blaming us. It's a textbook emotional reaction."

The sun was starting to cook them alive. It was a relief when Val pulled onto the main road and picked up some speed. Michelle shut her eyes and took in the breeze.

"Are you speaking from experience, my friend?" Val asked.

"No, absolutely not. Neil and I have had our problems, but he has never cheated on me."

Michelle opened her mouth, but quickly shut it. It was best to leave that one alone. Not cheating was a rather low standard, but it was no secret that Neil was not a model husband. It wasn't her business to comment.

"Lisa, try not to worry about it," Val said. "Think about the gourmet lunch that's waiting for us."

"I guess." She let out a groan. "Unless the police are already at the hotel. Do you think I can change out of this outfit before I go to jail?"

"Of course!"

Michelle was struck by how familiar this all felt: Val with her endless bravado, and Lisa with her spiraling anxiety. It wasn't a perfect match, but it worked.

"Justine would've loved that," she yelled over the wind.

Lisa turned around, the frown on her face finally breaking into a crooked smile. "You're right. She would've died laughing at you yelling at that woman."

Michelle nodded. She thought so, too.

●●●

They got back to the hotel in record time, thanks to Val's aggressive driving. They changed out of their cleaning outfits and their "butler" met them for lunch.

Michelle didn't like the butler situation at all. Apparently, being in the penthouse suite meant they got personalized attention. There was nothing more mortifying to Michelle than personalized attention.

Val and Lisa, however, thought having a butler was delightful. Lisa reacted to everything the guy said with oohing and aahing, like he was some sort of revelation. Val hit on him, and Michelle remained polite but awkward.

The lunch he'd arranged was exquisite. They started with Florida littleneck clams in a carrot vinaigrette, then moved on to a smoked mahi-mahi salad with fried plantain chips. Next up were truffle jalapeño fritters, followed by an option of either Chilean sea bass or ricotta and butternut squash agnolotti. Dessert was a shared chocolate brownie with vanilla ice cream, toasted marshmallow, and a peanut butter ganache.

It was far, far too much, in that decadent way that was so rarely worth it. This time, however, it was worth every bite. Michelle told herself this as she took one last spoonful of brownie. She hadn't meant to stuff herself, but she couldn't help it. The food was too good, and the view of the ocean was too enchanting. For the first time on this entire escapade, she felt relaxed.

Val sat back with a grunt, half of her plate untouched. "Fancy hotels, man. They know how to do it. But you know what?"

"What?" asked Lisa, polishing off the last of the melted ice cream.

"You get used to it *so* fast. You don't value nice things for long."

Lisa let out a sigh and adjusted her neon-pink visor. "I'd love a chance to get used to this." Apparently unsatisfied with her sun protection, she popped on her sunglasses, too. "You guys really don't think we'll get in trouble?"

"I'd like to see Lou try," Val said. "If he says anything, we'll just tell all the little Emerald Warriors about his secret family."

"That's honestly a good point," Michelle said. "He has a squeaky-clean image and acts like he's perfect to all those poor souls."

"He's just a liar," Lisa said, shaking her head. "At least Justine was honest. She never claimed to be perfect. She never tried."

"That's why he dumped her," Val said, sucking loudly on the straw in her empty drink.

The butler noticed immediately and ran off to the bar, returning with a replacement drink moments later.

"He's just one of those guys," Lisa said. "Nothing is ever enough for him."

Michelle nodded. "Amen."

After lunch, they were scheduled for a day at the spa. Michelle had never been to a spa and felt uncomfortable with the whole process. She didn't like getting undressed, she didn't like the overly calming music, and she didn't like walking around in flat, weird slippers and a borrowed fluffy robe.

How many people had worn this robe? What if they'd had scabies? Her skin was crawling.

Naturally, Lisa and Val didn't share her fears. They loved the rejuvenation facial and requested additional neck massages to go along with it. Michelle felt like the standard arm and hand massages were more than enough discomfort and declined any additions.

Then it was time for the full-body massages. Val opted for a terrifying-looking cupping massage, which she insisted would make her feel "reborn." Lisa got a standard Swedish massage, and Michelle asked for the one that had the least amount of touching. Her masseuse laughed, sure she was joking.

She was not. She ended up with a hot stone massage, and despite the first moments of awkwardness, after a few minutes of her muscles being pressed in just the right way, she felt herself forgetting her sheepishness and turning into a puddle.

Lastly, they had manicures and pedicures. Michelle didn't enjoy getting her nails done, but she was willing to try it since the massage had gone so well.

It took an hour, which was way too long, and it turned out she still didn't like having anyone touch her hands or feet. At least her nails looked lovely in a shining coral red.

When they were finally done with the spa, Michelle suggested they all go upstairs and take a nap, but Val wouldn't hear it. She insisted they needed to rent a cabana on the beach.

"It's too hot," Michelle said. The UV index was sky-high too. The sun would age them three years.

"Come on. It'll be fun," Val pleaded. "We can sit back and relax and watch the ocean."

Unfortunately, the butler overheard Val and ran over to tell her he'd already reserved the best cabana for them. Michelle felt bad turning him down, so she relented.

Val ended up being absolutely right. Under the shade of the bright yellow cabana, they could feel the breeze off the ocean while enjoying the view of the striking blue water.

"It's not the Maldives," Lisa said, "but it'll do."

Michelle laughed. Perhaps it was the two Mai Tais the butler had brought her, but this beach vacation was far more enjoyable than she'd expected. Their ever-attentive butler never appeared empty-handed. If he didn't have a drink, he'd show up with a tray of chilled strawberries, or ice-cold chocolates, or raspberry cake pops. It was like something out of a movie. Michelle was starting to see what Val meant about getting used to luxury.

She ended up being the only one who actually went into the ocean. The waves were surprisingly high, and she leapt and played, bodysurfing like a kid. It was the most fun she'd had in weeks. Months, maybe.

That night, they had dinner at a local Cuban restaurant. It wasn't fancy in the least, but the food was spectacular. It felt much more Justine-like than the hotel – the place was family-owned, down to earth, and genuine.

Afterwards, Michelle suggested they spread some of Justine's ashes at the beach. "She obviously loved this place if she wanted us to be here."

"You're right," said Val. "Let me get my candles."

"Candles?"

Val nodded, digging through her bag. "Yes. I brought a candle for us to light for her at every location. You know how she loved candles."

Lisa's face faded into a quivering frown. "She really did."

They made their way out on the beach, struggling to walk until they abandoned their shoes. The sand was oddly cold despite the heat of the day.

They reached the edge of the black ocean. They couldn't see any stars, and the wind was fierce, ripping through their clothes and hair. The waves had picked up enormously, crashing with a fury they hadn't seen during the day. The spray from the water sent a chill through Michelle's body.

Val struggled to light the candle until Lisa stepped in to block the wind.

When she'd finally lit it, she cleared her throat. "Here we lay to rest our beautiful friend, Justine Miller. She had all of the fun, color, and beauty of Miami in her soul, and was the most generous person we've ever known. Rest in peace, Justine. We love you."

Michelle opened the box and stuck her hand in, removing a handful of fine, sand-like ash. "We love you, girl."

Nine

The next morning, they were enjoying breakfast on their balcony when there was a call from the front desk.

Lisa answered, "Hello?"

It was the butler. "Hi. I'm so sorry to disturb you, but I believe you may have a visitor? It's actually for Miss Valerie Villano."

Michelle and Val had followed her inside and Lisa poked at the phone, trying to figure out how to put it on speaker. She finally found the right button. "Oh okay. Who is it?"

"She says her name is Chloe Evans. Is that someone you're expecting?"

Lisa dropped her plate onto the floor. Somehow, it didn't shatter. "I told you," she whispered. "We're going to get in trouble."

"I'm not here!" yelled Val.

The butler hesitated. "Yes, of course. I never confirmed you were here."

"Hang on," Michelle said. "Shouldn't we listen to what she has to say?"

"No!" Lisa said. "We should be trying to sneak out of here."

"Oh, stop." Michelle shook her head and leaned over the speaker. "Tell her we'll meet her in the café."

She ended the call and looked at her friends. "I'll go by myself if you two are too cowardly."

Valerie let out a sigh. "Fine, but if we get arrested, I'm not covering bail."

"Spoken like a true best friend," Michelle said with a smile.

"If you can confirm the police aren't involved," Lisa announced, "then I will consider joining you two."

It was a valiant effort, but Val and Michelle ridiculed her so badly that she relented in going downstairs with them.

It wasn't easy for Lisa. She felt dizzy and sweat had breached her shirt by the time they got down to the hotel lobby.

"I can't afford to get arrested," she whispered as they walked through.

Val didn't seem to have a care in the world. She kept peering at the expensive boutiques they passed. "Are you on parole or something?"

"No." Lisa hung back, peeking through the glass walls of the café. It was in a quiet corner of the hotel, and she could see everyone inside. The police could be hiding anywhere, though. In the bushes, undercover at the bar, or scuba-suited in the pool.

What kind of strings could Lou pull with the local police? What kind of resources did they have for him? Or maybe he had his own security...

Lisa wasn't on parole – of course not, she wouldn't have been able to travel if she were – but things at her job hadn't ended on the best terms. Her friends didn't need to know about that, though. It had all been a big misunderstanding. She didn't want to ruin the fun by explaining it. Except it wouldn't look good now if she was accused of breaking into a home.

Chloe stood from her seat and waved at them, and Michelle walked in without hesitation.

Lisa took a deep breath. It would all work out. It'd be fine. She could slip through the back door, run onto the beach, and disappear if necessary.

"Thanks for meeting me," Chloe said.

She didn't look angry or anything – maybe a bit nervous. Was she looking over her shoulder because she expected someone?

Could be. Lisa checked the exits.

"We're happy to," Michelle said, taking the lead. She reached out and shook Chloe's hand. "I'm Michelle."

Chloe nodded. "I know. I figured it out after you guys left. I recognized Valerie first. I've always been a fan."

"Thank you." Val waved a hand, as if to say "oh stop."

Lisa decided it was best not to introduce herself. Perhaps Chloe didn't know her name yet. No need to flaunt it.

They took their seats and she studied the girl. She wasn't a girl, of course, though she looked to be about Sierra's age. Perhaps a bit older. It was hard for Lisa to tell anymore.

Sometimes she forgot and had to remind herself she wasn't twenty-one anymore. When would that go away? When would she get used to being closer to Medicare age than to being newly able to drink?

Whatever her age, Chloe was stunning, with her shining chestnut curls and smooth, tanned skin. Her teeth were perfectly straight and shockingly white, likely the result of braces from parents who loved her dearly. How did they feel about their daughter dating a man twice her age?

"How did you find us?" Val asked.

"Oh." Chloe reached into her purse and pulled out a black-and-white picture of the three of them. "I got this from the doorbell cam."

Michelle pulled the picture closer. "Doorbell cam, huh?"

"Don't worry. I erased the footage," Chloe said. "I looked at it after you'd left. I was just so stunned I didn't realize who I was talking to at the time."

"I am sorry about all that," Val said as she picked up a menu. "At least now you know Lou's a dog."

Lisa let out a sigh. "Don't bring dogs into this. Lou should be so lucky. He has no loyalty."

Chloe flinched, and Lisa immediately felt bad about what she'd said. She rushed to correct herself. "I'm sorry. It's too soon, isn't it? We just – "

Chloe shook her head. "No, it's not too soon. It's way overdue, actually." She paused and cleared her throat before continuing. "I was sorry to hear about Justine. Lou didn't talk much about her, even when I would ask, but I knew her a bit through my early Emerald sessions. She was always so kind and welcoming and...yeah. Just a lovely person."

Lisa pinched her lips together. Chloe was a nice girl. She deserved much better than Lou.

"Thank you." Michelle said.

Chloe continued. "I met Lou after a friend convinced me to go to an Emerald recruitment event. I was struggling in my PhD program and felt like a failure. I went to this class and it was all about figuring out what you wanted in life and building confidence. It was so inspiring. Lou was so inspiring."

Val waved the waitress over. "Cappuccino, please." She turned to Chloe. "That's how they get you, isn't it? All that stuff was Justine's idea. She was always talking about positive energy and building the life you want."

Chloe nodded. "It was all positive at first. Later, when Lou and I started dating, he wanted to keep it quiet. I should have been suspicious then but...." She groaned. "I'm an idiot, I guess."

Lisa let out a *tsk*. "You're not an idiot. Lou is much older than you and quite a skilled manipulator."

"The woman in the painting is an Emerald Elite," Chloe said. "I've taken classes from her. She's *nice*. I don't know why

Lou would do this. I don't know why she would lie. It feels like my life has fallen apart over the last twenty-four hours."

Lisa didn't know what to tell this girl. At least she hadn't married the guy, but that wouldn't be much of a comfort now.

Michelle had an idea, it seemed. "You know, we don't hate Lou. We were all friends once. But we've watched Justine's vision become more corrupted over the years."

"Even when Justine couldn't see it," Val added. She took a sip of the cappuccino that had just arrived. "You can't really blame yourself. At least you're out of it and now you can make him pay."

Chloe laughed, but Michelle and Lisa exchanged glances. They knew Val wasn't joking.

"I've been blind to it for so long," Chloe said. "I dropped out of my program and dedicated myself to the Path of the Emerald. I was convinced it was the only way to find happiness, and some of it did make me feel better. Well, not the sessions so much. They were really expensive, but the *community* is so great. I made so many friends. But I started to get the feeling that something wasn't right a few months ago."

"You poor thing," Lisa said. She no longer feared being arrested and could finally feel for this girl. "You can't let him hold you back. Let this be the last time Lou Emerald ruins your day."

"Hang on," Val said, holding up a finger. "Wouldn't you like to get back at him?"

"Val," Michelle said, voice full of warning.

"What?" Val shrugged. "The only thing that could make a breakup sweeter is a little revenge."

Chloe looked at her, eyes wide. "Uh..."

Val leaned in. "Have you broken up with him yet?"

Chloe shook her head. "Not yet, but I will. I think I was in shock."

"Don't do it quite yet," Val said, ignoring Michelle's glare. "You might be able to help us. I mean, if you want to."

"Val," Lisa said, "don't drag her into this." She was already full of regret for going along with Val's plan. Chloe didn't need to be a part of it, too.

"Help you do what, exactly?"

Val smiled brightly. "It's come to our attention that – "

Michelle cut her off. "No, Val. Just stop."

Chloe's eyes darted between them. "I'd like to help. If I can."

The thought of saying Val's theory out loud was suddenly mortifying to Lisa. She interrupted Val just as she started to speak. "We think there are some things Lou might've been dishonest about. About Justine, and about the divorce."

Val narrowed her eyes, but said nothing about being silenced.

"What kind of things?" asked Chloe. "Like assets?"

"Sort of," Michelle said. "But you don't want to get involved. Trust me."

Chloe sat back and crossed her arms. "No, I think I do. Let me help. Please."

Lisa felt like she was watching a game of high-stakes poker. She was terrible at poker. Neil never let her play when he had his friends over.

"All right," Val said. "We're looking for information. Do you have access to Lou's house in Santa Monica? The one he shared with Justine?"

She nodded. "Of course. I have access to all of his homes. There are cameras there, too, though."

"Val," Michelle said, dropping her voice, "We are not doing this again."

"I'll invite you," Chloe said. "As my guests. I can disable the cameras when I'm there, too. When did you want to go?"

A smile spread across Val's face. "How's tomorrow?"

Ten

They were supposed to spend their last night in Miami relaxing, but Michelle wouldn't allow it. She tried to cut dinner short so they could get back to the hotel and pack their bags to be ready for the morning.

"Our flight isn't until ten-thirty," Val complained. "I'm pretty sure we're not going to miss it."

Michelle wasn't having it. "With that attitude, we might."

Val tried to let it go, she really did. She made no comments at dinner, ignoring Michelle's heavy sighs and glances at her watch as they waited for the check. When Michelle offered to drive them home "to make it easier," she held her tongue and handed over the keys.

Val still managed to have a good time with Lisa, and when they got back to the hotel, she dutifully packed her bags just as Michelle told her to. She also agreed to get to the airport three hours early, despite the fact that there was no need for it, and it caused them to miss brunch at the hotel.

She told herself it was all fine. They returned the car and got through security in a record-breaking twenty-six minutes. Val thought she had been more than tolerant of Michelle's rules and, hoping to savor Miami for a few last hours, suggested they pop into a restaurant for brunch and a drink.

Michelle looked at her like she'd just suggested stripping naked and running through the terminal. "What? Absolutely not. We need to be at the gate."

Now she'd gone too far. "At the *gate?* We have almost two hours before the flight and – "

"There could be changes, it could come early, it – "

"Right," Val scoffed, "because lots of planes come early and then leave without telling any of the passengers."

"Ladies," Lisa said slowly, "there's no need to argue. I'll go to the gate and call you if there are changes, okay? I don't mind."

"I never said I wanted brunch," Michelle snapped. "We have a long flight. I don't need to load up on greasy food beforehand and feel sick the whole time."

Val turned so Michelle couldn't see her rolling her eyes. "Okay!" she called out. "I'll be getting brunch if anyone wants to join me."

She eyed the menu of a place nearby called The Blue Wave Flame. It was horribly overpriced, but she didn't care. They had a credit card from Zora for all of their expenses. It didn't seem like anywhere else was open, and the place had Cuban sliders. That was fun.

"Enjoy." Michelle walked off, clutching her rolling bag tightly.

Val turned to Lisa. "Are you hungry?"

A look of panic crossed her face. "No, I'm okay. I think I'll just go sit with her. I know she's nervous about the flight."

"All right."

"Unless you're upset? I can join you for a little while."

Oh, sweet Lisa. Still trying to make everyone happy. Val thought she'd grow out of that, but it seemed she'd only grown into it.

Val smiled and shook her head. "Seriously, don't worry about it. I can bring you something?"

"Nah, I'm okay. See you soon!" Lisa rushed off, chasing after Michelle.

That was fine. It would be good to have alone time. Healthy, even.

Val walked into the restaurant and took a seat at the bar. There was only one other patron at this time of day, so she struck up a conversation with him. He was traveling for business, which she hadn't expected since he was so sloppily dressed. What was it with people wearing sweatpants everywhere they went? Were jeans *that* uncomfortable?

He was interesting enough, though, at least for brunch. His company arranged study abroad trips for students, and he was more than happy to tell her about all his travels.

He droned on and her mind drifted. Maybe Michelle wouldn't be so uptight about flying if she had studied abroad in college. Or maybe she'd be less uptight in general if she'd finished college, or ever tried leaving the island!

These thoughts whirled and simmered through two drinks with Mr. Travel Guy, which was extended by a forty-five-minute flight delay.

Val arrived at the gate before the plane did. Michelle said hello, and Val said hello back. She thought perhaps Michelle had had some time to cool down, but as they boarded, it became obvious Michelle's mood had only worsened. Lisa was frantically upbeat, trying to balance the mood.

Once in their seats, Val ordered champagne for them all. Michelle declined hers and instead focused on getting all of her flying supplies ready: her neck pillow, chapstick, hand sanitizer, water bottle, and blanket.

Oh well, her loss. "This is to celebrate our successful first steps into investigating Lou."

Michelle shot her a disgusted look. "How can you drink this early?"

The smile on Lisa's face dipped along with her champagne glass.

Val narrowed her eyes.

She should have recognized that her friend was simply nervous about the flight, and that Michelle wasn't perfect. Val should've seen Michelle's comments and controlling impulses for what they were: a product of her overwhelming flight-related anxiety.

But Val wasn't perfect, either, so instead of being understanding, she went with, "Maybe if you had a few drinks, you wouldn't be so annoying to fly with."

Michelle stopped struggling with her seat belt. "I never even wanted to fly in the first place!"

"Yeah, no kidding. Why go anywhere or experience anything when you can live your entire life on a tiny island?"

Lisa unbuckled herself and stood up. "How about we switch seats? I know you like the window, Val."

"Sure," she replied. "If that's what you want."

The rest of the flight proceeded without incident. Val felt bad about what she'd said almost immediately, but she couldn't stop herself for some reason. They were behaving like teenagers again. It was silly.

Michelle wasn't to blame, not really. The root of the matter was that Reggie used to nag Val in a similar way, telling her she was being irresponsible, or making them late, or he'd twist everything into being her fault, even when he spilled his own coffee on himself. It drove her nuts, and it made her feel like she was always in the wrong.

She'd lived under his negativity for too long, but that was no excuse. It was just an explanation for how she'd acted.

When they finally got off the plane at LAX, Val offered her a sheepish apology. "I'm sorry about what I said."

"It's okay." Michelle let out a sigh. "I'm sorry I terrorized you. I'll be normal now. At least until we fly back to the East Coast."

Val felt the need to explain. "Reggie used to always get mad at me when we traveled for shows. He made everything a big deal and...I don't know. I think I'm overly sensitive."

"No, I'm overly sensitive," Michelle said. "Because a small part of me is convinced we won't survive every plane ride, so I try to control every factor I can."

Lisa laughed. "Oh, you two. Two sensitive old women."

"Hey!" Val barked. "Who are you calling old?"

"Yeah!" Michelle added. "You better not mean us."

Lisa put her hands up in an apparent surrender. "Of course not! I was talking about two old women over there, not you two."

Michelle nodded. "Right."

It felt so much better once the air was cleared. Traveling was always more stressful than Val remembered. Memories of complications and stress softened with time, but pictures from trips never faded. It was those lovely, enchanting pictures of past travels that lured her to try again.

"Next time I'll offer you four Benadryl and a blindfold so you don't have to worry," she said.

Michelle cracked a smile. "Thanks. That would really help."

The drive to The Henge Hotel was complicated by the usual Los Angeles traffic. Lisa, seemingly trying to avoid another spat, filled the silence with observations.

"I don't know how you can stand it. Seattle traffic can be bad, but this seems like another level."

Val shrugged. "You get used to it. Los Angeles more than makes up for it with the rest of her charms. The food, the people, the opportunities!"

"The opportunities!" Lisa clapped her hands together. "I wonder what opportunities we'll have."

"The chance to get arrested?" Michelle suggested.

Lisa shook her head. "No, not like that. I meant like the chance to see a celebrity."

"Who do you want to see?"

She paused, deep in thought, before saying, "Paul Rudd."

Val laughed. "Still running on that *Clueless* crush?"

"Yes, but he's done a lot of things since *Clueless*," Lisa said matter-of-factly. "And he seems like the nicest guy. Though I guess I wouldn't want to bother him. I'd just like to see him, you know? From afar."

"Lisa's going to try to crawl into Paul Rudd's house," Michelle said with a laugh.

"I am not! I am going to crawl into Lou's house."

"Ugh. Don't remind me." Michelle peered out the window. "What else has been going on with you out here, Val?"

She shrugged. "I was asked to teach a few lectures at Loyola."

Lisa's jaw dropped. "That's so neat! Did you do it?"

Val let out a sigh. Lisa would find that exciting. It was nothing, though. Really nothing. "I did, and it was fun, but it's not for me."

"Why not?"

"Teaching is for has-beens. Plus, those kids aren't serious about music. They asked me to come back full time and – "

"Val!" Michelle turned to her, all stern and serious-faced. "This is a great opportunity. You should at least consider it."

She waved a hand. "My best days are still ahead of me. Now that I'm getting rid of Reggie, I can finally take full control of my career."

Lisa turned around from the backseat. "I have to ask. Who gets your LA mansion in the divorce?"

"No one," Val said with a laugh. The truth was they'd had to sell that off years ago. When her album sales dried up, so did all of her opportunities to perform. Their cash flow abruptly stopped, which was quite rude of it to do, considering how costly their lives had become. The house, along with other things they'd gotten used to, was just too expensive to keep.

She missed it sometimes, but that was all in the past. Her one-bedroom apartment was cozy enough, even if it wasn't fancy. At least she wasn't worried about it being broken into while she traveled. Low maintenance was good. The mansion was never low maintenance.

"Where are you staying now? Can we see it?" asked Michelle.

"Nah, you don't want to waste your time there. My place is way across town."

Their fear of traffic was enough to get them to stop asking, and once they saw The Henge Hotel, Val's dinky apartment was far from their minds.

It was pure Californian luxury. Unlike the glitzy Ocean Drive in Miami, the hotels off of Santa Monica's Ocean Ave basked in a more low-key glamour. There was an old money feel, without the need to show off with flashing lights.

The Henge Hotel was the picture of Mediterranean Revival architecture: the red clay roof, white stucco walls, and casual patios blended seamlessly into the ocean landscape. It was one of the few hotels that was oceanside of the road, standing a humble four floors tall, unlike their previous hotel high rise.

The hotel kept a smattering of cabanas and villas near the sand. The pool was tasteful, with a gradual sloped entry that gave it the feel of a beautiful lagoon. If the Hotel Lusso had been an electric yellow Lamborghini, the Henge Hotel was an eggshell Aston Martin with gold trim.

They didn't have the penthouse suite this time, but only because there was no penthouse. Instead, they had an ocean view villa, with easy access to the Ocean Front Walk.

They were in the middle of the action, close to all of the best restaurants, and an easy drive from the hustle of Hollywood Boulevard. Zora had offered to arrange tickets for a show, but they opted instead to do one of Justine's favorite activities: walk the Santa Monica Pier.

Their earlier spat was a distant memory. They walked, three across, sampling the various Justine-approved delicacies Lou had never liked: corn dogs, chocolate-covered popcorn, churros, and tamales.

Lisa managed to convince them to ride the Ferris wheel, and up they went, one hundred and thirty feet above the pier. The screams of children on the rides below faded into the wind and they watched revelers on the beach.

Afterwards, Val convinced them to make the walk from the pier to the Venice Beach Boardwalk. It was easy enough to do. The weather was a perfect seventy-three degrees, and there were hundreds of opportunities for people watching, another Justine favorite.

Lisa in particular liked the Muscle Beach Outdoor Gym. "This is just how it looks in the movies!" she gushed. "I can't believe it's real!"

A shirtless man with a particularly shiny chest winked at her. "Believe me, it's real."

She squealed, turning away from him with her mouth hanging open. "Let's move," she said, cheeks red.

"Why?" Val asked. "I like his muscles. Hey!" She waved. "How strong are you?"

He smiled. "How strong do you need me to be?"

Even Michelle giggled at that, and they rushed off like a gaggle of school girls.

It was fun to be with her high school friends again. Something about it made her feel young. They had known her way back when, and even with all the years between them, it felt like they still knew each other. They knew the parts that mattered, at least.

Further down the boardwalk, they stopped to admire some murals and enjoy a few street performances: tumblers, beat boxers, a skate boarding dog, and a man walking on broken glass. Michelle and Lisa were mesmerized.

Val loved bringing tourists here. It was so lively, so fun. She and Justine would sometimes meet up at the pier or along the boardwalk. Justine loved watching the people – she loved seeing them happy. People flocked to her, too. They couldn't go to a restaurant without the waiter becoming her best friend. She was just that sort of person.

"Hey!" Val waved them away from a souvenir store. "One of Justine's favorite bars is coming up. It's a hole-in-the-wall type place. The bartender is this old sailor who tells tales about shipwrecks and gives out stern advice."

"You had me at 'Justine's favorite,'" Lisa said.

Michelle smiled. She looked so much more relaxed. "And you had me at stern advice."

Val laughed. It was good to get their fun out of the way now. Tomorrow, Chloe would arrive and they'd need to get down to business. "This way!"

Eleven

There was no stopping Val. Michelle was starting to understand that, and after their carefree romp at the seaside, she decided to take a page out of Justine's book and just go with it.

If only she'd learned to go with the flow sooner. She might have come to visit LA before. Justine had invited her so many times. Why hadn't she made the time? Why had she allowed herself to put her life on hold like that?

It still didn't seem real that Justine was gone. How could she be here one moment, and the next moment just...disappear? She'd had so much life in her, so much energy and love. Where was it now? Where did it all go?

These thoughts plagued her as she drifted off to sleep and reappeared the moment she awoke in that luxurious hotel bed. She sat up and the smell of fresh coffee drifted in. She could hear Val trying to be quiet as she bumped around just outside her door.

Michelle stood and pulled the curtains open. The beach filled the frame of the window. Another beautiful day at a beautiful hotel, in this charming and lively city by the sea. It was all perfect, except for the cold, hard fact that Justine wasn't there to enjoy it. She'd wanted them to experience all of this, the fun and the fights that made up *togetherness*.

The urge to dissolve into tears and ruin the perfectly white fluffy towels with her leftover mascara rushed over her. She wanted this moment to actually be perfect. She wanted Justine to walk through the door so she could tell her about what they'd seen and done.

But it couldn't happen. It would never happen again.

It was always in these quiet moments that grief snuck in, bubbling up, a bittersweet reminder of what could have been but was now forever lost. Grief was learning to live with forever, one moment at a time.

Michelle didn't allow herself to break down. Not this time. She still had Val and Lisa. They had each other, and they had this moment.

Her phone went off with a message from Arthur. "Hope you're not getting too cool for us out in LA. We're getting some rain, which is nice. Everything at the cafe is running smoothly, so don't worry about that, but we do miss you."

That was nice. She smiled, brushed away a tear, and prepared for whatever chaos the day would bring.

● ● ●

It began at breakfast.

Val dropped her fork onto her plate with an alarming clang. "Chloe messaged me!"

Michelle looked up from her breakfast tacos. At least they would be guests during this invasion, instead of fake employees. That seemed like a step up.

"She said she was able to disable all of the cameras, but she's not sure if there's one in the front she doesn't have access to." Val nodded, a pleased look on her face. "She asked that we enter from the beach and take the back stairs."

All right, so they had to sneak in. Legally, they were still guests, but it was getting murkier.

Michelle took her last bite of food and spoke up. "That's fine, but can we agree on something? If we don't find anything at this house, we stop there? Let Justine rest in peace?"

"How can she rest in peace when her husband plotted to murder her and got away with it?" Val shot back, arms crossed.

Lisa downed the rest of her mimosa. "To be fair, I don't think she cares much now."

Lisa had a point, and for her to speak up and say anything was significant. She was terribly non-confrontational, and at times it was hard to tell what she even wanted.

The Miami trespass had excited her, but this time she had been much quieter. Michelle guessed her fear of getting in trouble was winning over her need for adventure.

This was all Val's fight. She slipped her phone into her purse and sat back. "Well, I care. You don't have to come, but I'd like you to."

"Do I have to come?" Michelle asked with a wry smile.

"I'm not forcing you to, no." Val shrugged. "Though I will remind you, dear Michelle, that last time you were the key player in finding out about Lou's secret family. You are a valued member of this team."

"What about me?" Lisa asked. "Aren't I a valued member?"

Val reached over and put her hand on top of Lisa's. "Of course you are! I want you to be there. I need you to be there, but I'm giving you an easy way out. No hard feelings."

A small smile crossed Lisa's face.

Ah, there it was. *That* was how Lisa felt. She didn't care either way; she just wanted to be wanted.

"I'm in," Lisa said, pouring herself a second mimosa. "I'd like to see this place."

Michelle closed her eyes for a moment. She knew she could go back to the hotel and sit in a cabana by the pool. The white linen curtains would blow in the breeze and she could watch the passersby. She could rent a bicycle and eat churros!

She could do anything other than scrounge around a mansion owned by a man she didn't believe was a murderer.

She had no real choice, though.

It was going to be a long day.

After breakfast, they followed Chloe's directions and parked two streets away from the house. The neighborhood was quiet and filled with enormous houses. There were no people outside except the ones working on the landscaping.

They parked, then wove through the expensive cars unnoticed until finding a path that led down to the beach.

Val charged ahead, her mood manic, her eyes wild. "See Michelle? This is turning into a hike, just like you like!"

"Is this a hike?"

Val paused. "No, I guess you're right. You can't hike in rich people neighborhoods. They call the cops."

"Aw man, really?" Lisa was a few yards behind them, struggling to keep up. Her strappy sandals were acting as sand shovels and slowing her down.

Michelle had taken off her flip-flops, choosing to walk closer to the water. The wet sand was much easier to walk on, and she loved the feeling of being kissed by the freezing sea.

"That's it, up there." Val pointed to a house that looked like it was hanging off the cliff above.

"How many stairs is that?" asked Lisa. "It doesn't look safe, honestly."

Val laughed. "Oh, come on. It's safe! I'll go first."

Off she went, power-walking the stairs, taking them two at a time. Michelle and Lisa followed slowly but steadily behind.

Once Val reached the top, she turned to cheer them on. "You can do it! Wait until you see this view! I feel like an eagle!"

"What kind of eagle bullies her friends into doing things they don't want to do?" asked Lisa.

Michelle laughed, coughing from her breathlessness. She was used to hiking, but something about this was making her winded. Maybe it was the anxiety. "All of them, I think. Birds are pushy."

Lisa nodded, clinging to the handrail for a moment before tackling the last flight. "She's definitely an eagle, then. Or maybe a pigeon."

"A pigeon-eagle."

"Is that a thing?"

"Yes," Michelle lied, but her face betrayed her. Lisa shot her a look before turning and trudging up the rest of the stairs.

They made it into the backyard and spotted Chloe by the pool. She waved wildly with both hands.

Michelle waved back. She felt bad for the girl. If Lou found out what she was up to, he would surely get angry. He wouldn't hurt her...or would he?

No, not like that. He could cut her off from the Emerald community like he did Justine. That would hurt her. But it seemed she was well on her way to doing that herself.

"Hey!" Chloe yelled. "I'm so glad you made it. Come on in."

Val didn't need to be asked twice. She was right behind Chloe, chattering away. Lisa followed, and even Michelle had to admit she was curious to see what this house looked like.

They walked into the two-story living room, their voices echoing off the empty walls. It was an ugly sort of house, all concrete and glass. Some people liked that modern look, but Michelle wasn't one of them. The windows were like big, soulless cubes cut out of stone.

Even the shaggy rug in the center of the enormous room didn't make it look any less bleak. It was cold, like Justine had never been here.

"Sorry about this. It took me longer than expected to turn off all the cameras, but we're good now. You're free to look wherever you like."

Michelle raised an eyebrow. "Really? Anywhere?"

Chloe nodded. "Anywhere!"

"Do you have any recommendations?" Lisa asked.

Chloe bit her lip. "It depends on what you're looking for. I can check his computer. He thinks he's really smart because he makes me use my own account, but he keeps all of his passwords in a little black book by the desk. I can access almost anything."

Oh, shoot. Michelle did the same thing at home. Hopefully no one got into her house with the malicious intent of logging into her utilities or paying off her mortgage.

"I'll come with you," Lisa announced. "I need to make up for my poor performance at the last house."

Chloe laughed. "Sure."

"I'll be upstairs," Val said. "This place isn't as big as I expected it to be. Shouldn't take long."

Michelle let out a sigh. "I guess I'll wander around down here."

Michelle started her rounds, but her heart wasn't in it. The barren living room didn't have much to look through – just a TV and some fairly empty shelves.

She was able to flip through the ten books that were on display. It didn't seem like they were ever actually read. It was more like they were there to signal to guests what kind of person Lou was. All of them were about the power of positive thinking and the importance of not eating carbohydrates.

Why was it always a war on carbs?

The kitchen was a sight to behold, thirty feet across with an enormous cement island, muted gray cabinets, and a wine cellar the size of her bedroom. Michelle spent too much time browsing the bottles and admiring the organization of the pantry on the other side of the kitchen.

Perhaps she'd introduce some of the minimalism into her own home when she got back. This place was too empty, but her house was too full. Cluttered. A lot of it was her parents' old stuff, things she didn't want to throw away but never used. Maybe it was time to find them a new home.

She was tempted to grab a bottle of water from the fridge, but decided against it. Best not to leave their mark.

It looked so fancy, though, standing there in its tall glass bottle. Was that Lou's doing? Or Justine's? Justine wouldn't have opted for such a fancy option, unless she was trying to cut plastic waste. Lou would've wanted it for a different reason – to show how rich he was.

One bottle wouldn't hurt. She reopened the fridge and unscrewed the top, savoring her first sip.

It tasted like regular old water. A little grainy. Did they add minerals to it or something?

Gross.

She kept sipping it as she entered the next space, the game room. There were billiards, a poker table, and what looked like cigar-smoking chairs. An enormous TV took up most of the side wall, and there was a fully stocked bar that looked like it belonged in a boutique hotel. This wasn't a game room. It was a man cave.

Also gross.

So much delicate glass, too. If Lou's secret son got loose in this room, he could do a lot of damage.

Michelle smiled to herself. Oh yes, Lou's son could bring this concrete palace to its knees. Obviously, Lou would never allow him, or any child, into this home.

He probably had never changed a diaper, either. That seemed like the kind of father Lou Emerald was, despite the humble and hardworking image he presented to his devout followers.

Lisa yelled something, but Michelle could barely hear her. The thick walls were at least good for muting sound. She abandoned the man cave and headed to the office. "What's up?"

"We found something," Lisa said, eyes wide. "Well, Chloe found something."

"Oh yeah?"

Chloe looked at her, lips pressed into a thin line. "I'm not sure what to make of it. It's an email about a payout, I think? An insurance payout."

Michelle's heart sunk. "What?"

Val ran in, almost prancing and breathless. "What did I miss?"

"Chloe found an insurance payout," Lisa said quickly. "It looks like Tammy was right."

"I knew it!" Val pointed a finger at them. "A life insurance policy. How much?"

Chloe scrolled down. "Looks like just under two million dollars. I don't know why he'd do that, though. He has plenty of money. Two million is nothing to him."

"Unless he ran into trouble!" Val said, nodding. "Can you print that off? I'd like a copy."

Chloe shrugged. "Sure, if you'd like. I just don't understand. Why would he have taken out a life insurance policy on his ex-wife?"

Oh boy. They were getting dangerously close to telling Chloe about Val's crazy suspicions. Michelle needed to cut in. "Justine's mom kept insisting he had an insurance policy on her. She's struggling with her grief, you know? She suspects something malicious."

Chloe nodded. "Oh. Okay."

Michelle continued. "It's not uncommon to get an insurance policy before a divorce, then forget to cancel it. I think when we show Tammy how small the amount was, relative to Lou's net worth, it may calm some of her fears."

Chloe grabbed the paper off of the printer and handed it to Val. "What fears, exactly?"

Val folded it and tucked it into her purse. "That he had her killed."

"Valerie." Michelle shut her eyes. "You can't just go making accusations like that."

"Come on. Everyone's thinking it!"

Lisa made a face. "I mean, I wasn't thinking it before, but now I'm thinking it."

Michelle put up a hand. "No. Stop. I wish I'd had one before my husband died. I would've been able to stay in my house, for one thing." She turned to Chloe. "I don't think Lou is a killer. Don't worry."

Chloe let out a nervous laugh. "That's good. I would like to avoid being killed if at all possible."

Val put her arm around Chloe and put on her serious face. "Have you ever worried that he might kill you?"

"Not until now."

Lisa laughed, clearly trying to break the tension. "I don't think you have to worry. Just leave that loser behind."

"Wait." Val, apparently done with pretending she was Chloe's therapist, plopped herself into the computer chair. "Are there any other emails we can see?"

"He has a lot of emails," Chloe said with a shrug.

"What about around the time Justine died? Can we get into his phone records?"

"I don't have that kind of access," Chloe said. "I can look in the trash folder and see if there was anything he was trying to erase."

"That's a good idea," Lisa said. "I wish I'd come up with it."

Chloe clicked over and slowly scrolled down. "Spam, junk mail...fan mail...something from me. That's rude. He said he never got that."

Michelle bit her lip. The man was an adulterer and a glutton, but lying about an email Chloe had sent him was a new low, apparently.

"Hang on." Chloe clicked on an email. "This is weird. I don't know who this is."

"What does that say?" asked Lisa. "Oh. That's an angry one. It looks like a threat."

Val leaned in, reading aloud. "'Dear Mr. Emerald, I guess your price tag for your Bar Harbor story getting out is less than a hundred thousand dollars. Good luck with that.' It's signed 'Your boy SB.'"

"What do you think that's about?" Lisa asked.

This was getting silly. Lou probably got threatened and blackmailed all the time, especially with his unscrupulous morals. "Probably another secret family. Who knows?"

Val shook her head. "No, this email is from a guy. Someone named Sam Beverly."

"Sam could be a woman," Lisa argued.

"The picture is clearly of a man. Not even a man—a teenager."

Michelle leaned in. She was right. "Okay, I think we've gotten enough information for the day. We'd better get going before the tide comes in and we have to swim back. Thanks for your help, Chloe."

Chloe nodded, her eyes distant. "Any time."

Val patted her on the shoulder. "Hey, keep in touch, okay? If you need any showbiz advice, I'm your woman."

They left Chloe to grapple with what they'd found and exited through the backyard. Thankfully, going down the stairs was much easier than going up. The gorgeous view of the coast helped, as well as the relief that they were finally leaving.

Michelle wanted to reiterate how low the insurance payout was, but she couldn't get a word in. The excited chatter between Val and Lisa told Michelle all she needed to know. Their dumb murder theory had just gotten dumber, and she was the last one clinging onto any semblance of reality.

Twelve

The walk back to the car was steeper than Lisa remembered. She fell behind again, but this time she wasn't in a hurry to catch up. They weren't rushing now. They'd found what they needed, and as much as she hated to believe it, Val seemed to be on to something.

Her phone rang, and she waved Michelle and Val on, welcoming the excuse to take a break and enjoy the view for a moment more.

She turned to face the sea, seagulls squawking overhead. "Hello?"

"Hey, Mom. It's me."

"Hi Sierra! How are you?"

"I'm good. How's your trip?"

"It's wonderful." Lisa let out a long breath. The view really was incredible here. That was probably what Justine liked most. "I need to send you a picture of the beach I'm on now. Did you get my pictures from this morning?"

"Yeah, it looks fancy. You should start an Instagram account for your travels."

"Yeah right, just what I need. How'd your review go?"

Sierra let out a sigh. "My boss pushed it back until next week. Which is fine, because now I'll have more time to build my case for a promotion."

"Well that's a good attitude." Lisa smiled to herself. Her daughter was much more of a go-getter than she ever was.

Lisa had no idea where she'd gotten it. Sierra just came out that way. She was bold, confident, and *so* stubborn, even from a young age. It served her well now, though it had caused years of battles between them in her teenage years.

"Yeah. Um...is everything okay with Dad?"

Lisa's stomach tightened. She always kept the kids out of their father's troubles. "Of course. Why?"

"He called me and was acting strange."

Ugh. "Oh? Strange how?"

"For starters, he made it sound like your credit card got canceled and you wouldn't be able to get back from LA unless I sent money over."

Lisa shut her eyes, forcing her voice to sound carefree and light. "What? Oh, he's such a panicker. Just regular credit card stuff. You know how it is when you travel. I'm fine. We don't need your money, sweetie! Don't take him seriously."

"I never do," Sierra said with a laugh. "Okay, well, I'm glad you're having fun. I've got to go. Talk to you later!"

"Love you!"

"Love you too!"

She'd lost sight of Val and Michelle. Lisa cast one last look at the water before catching up to them.

"Everything okay?" Michelle asked.

"Oh, yeah, that was Sierra. I actually need to call Neil, if you don't mind waiting?"

Val nodded. "We'll be in the car. I need some alone time with Michelle to convince her anyway."

"Ah, yes, good." Lisa nodded. "I'll be right there."

Once they were out of earshot, Lisa called Neil once, then a second time.

The first time it rang for a while before going to voicemail. The second time, it went straight to voicemail.

He was ignoring her. Typical.

What was he thinking, trying to get money from his own child? That was a new low.

Neil had a history of lows, though. His gambling addiction had cost them a lot over the years – apartments, the only new car they'd ever laid their hands on, even Lisa's engagement ring. Most recently, Neil's addiction had cost Lisa her job.

What a mess that had been. She couldn't even think about it, it was so embarrassing. She'd been an accountant at the firm for nineteen years. They loved her, and she loved them. They trusted her with everything, all of the accounts, even giving her control over the slush fund.

Then money started disappearing. At first, it was only a few hundred here and there. She thought it was odd, and assumed the owners hadn't had time to catch her up on their expenses. Then, in one week, nearly eight thousand dollars disappeared overnight.

Somehow, Lisa's digital fingerprints were all over the transactions. She thought she was losing her mind, sleepwalking, or that she must've been hacked.

And boy, had she been. It took a bit of figuring, but she discovered that Neil had installed a keylogger on her computer. He saw every word she typed, every username, every password...

After the fallout, he promised to start going to Gamblers Anonymous meetings. He said he was going to get serious this time.

Was he going to say he didn't have the time? That was a lie.

He hadn't been able to keep a job in months, but apparently he had time to solicit money from Sierra.

They didn't need her money. Yes, they'd drained their savings to cover the losses, but they still had enough coming in to cover their bills. Her company had graciously given her a severance package. That would last two more months, and Lisa had made sure she was the only one with access to the account.

She didn't tell him about that, actually. Hopefully he hadn't found out. He would throw a tantrum, crying and yelling, telling her she was being abusive and controlling.

She didn't want to be controlling! But they needed to keep some money safe to pay the bills. Lisa had left him in control of his credit card. Now she was afraid to check the balance.

She called him one last time, and again got his voicemail.

A car honk rang out and Lisa looked up to see Val hanging out of the driver's seat. "Hey, pretty lady! Need a ride?"

She laughed and shoved her phone into her pocket. She'd deal with Neil later. "Sure."

"Hop in!"

● ● ●

They got back to the hotel and changed. Lisa snuck out to the lobby and managed to pay for a cup of coffee with her credit card. That was a relief. At least it was still working.

She called the bank and discovered Neil had managed to charge more than his three-thousand-dollar limit. She'd only allowed it to be that high in case of emergencies. Otherwise, she'd trust him with no more than five hundred.

But here they went. *Another* three thousand dollars. Where was she going to get the money to pay for that?

She hated to freeze his card, but she didn't know what else to do. It was sometimes the only way to get him to talk to her. She authorized the freeze and silenced her phone. No need to ruin the day with that.

She returned to the room as Val and Michelle were getting ready for the next stop on their itinerary: The Huntington. It was a library, a museum, and a botanical garden.

Lisa had never heard of it, but apparently Justine adored it. She had loved walking the gardens and spending hours there.

They piled into the car and strolled into The Huntington as a jolly trio. Lisa was happy to be there and thought it sounded nice, but she figured a garden was a garden. She assumed they'd walk through and be done in twenty minutes.

She couldn't have been more wrong. There were a hundred and thirty acres of gardens. Even Val stopped her campaign about the insurance policy to admire the beauty around them.

Lisa felt like an aristocrat, smelling the flowers and walking around in the long dress she'd saved for Los Angeles. There were sixteen gardens, all with different themes. Lisa's favorite was the Japanese garden with its bonsai trees and ceremonial teahouse. Michelle, ever the biologist, loved the lily ponds, and Val favored the twelve hundred varieties in the rose garden.

Dinner was on the other side of town at a Somali restaurant, another of Justine's favorites. It didn't look fancy on the inside, and Lisa had no idea what she was ordering when she picked the "chicken and rice plate" as her meal.

Val mentioned Justine's name and the owner asked where she'd been. They broke the bad news, and he looked genuinely sad. "One of the nicest ladies we ever had around here," he said.

Wasn't that the truth. Whether by association with Justine or just the normal operation of the restaurant, Lisa's meal came out with enormous portions of rice, chicken and vegetables. Everything was spiced to perfection and drizzled with a heavenly sauce that tied it together beautifully.

Lisa was reminded of the time Justine had visited her two years prior. They'd decided to go apple picking north of the city, and Justine had gotten caught speeding. Somehow, despite being twenty-five over the limit, she managed to talk her way down to a warning.

Lisa had never seen anything like it. She could never get out of trouble, but Justine had this charm that people responded to. It wasn't even that she was trying to get out of the ticket; she'd made the cop laugh so hard he told them to get out of his sight.

When they got up to leave, the restaurant owner stopped them. "Here," he said, pushing a container into Val's hands. "This was Justine's favorite dessert. Take it. Enjoy. We will miss her."

Lisa felt herself starting to lose it, so she excused herself to head outside.

• • •

The next morning, they got breakfast at a cute little café near the hotel. It was all going well until Michelle spotted Chloe through the window.

"Valerie," Michelle said slowly, turning to her. "Did you neglect to tell us we'd be having another guest for breakfast?"

Val flashed a smile. "Oh, heh. I didn't know she was going to come. Chloe and I have been texting back and forth. I've been encouraging her to dump Lou and move on with her life. I might've mentioned that if she was in the neighborhood, she could stop by."

"And there she is," Lisa said quietly, catching Chloe's eye and waving her over.

"She might have some news for us," Val said, smiling a bright smile.

Michelle shook her head and took a sip of her banana mango smoothie. "I thought we agreed to let all of that go?"

"We agreed to let it go if we didn't find anything," Val corrected. "I'd say a multi-million-dollar life insurance payout is definitely something."

"What are we going to do?" Michelle asked in a hushed voice. "There aren't any more houses to break into, and if you do end up being successful in getting Chloe to dump Lou, you've lost your only 'in.'"

Chloe arrived at the edge of their table, a smile on her face. "Hi! It's nice to see you all again."

"Chloe, welcome!" Val stood and gave her a hug. "Have a seat. Have you eaten yet?"

"Not yet," she said, voice small. "I don't mean to crash your breakfast."

"Oh please, you're always welcome," Val said with a smile.

The waitress stopped by and took Chloe's order – black coffee. "I won't stay long. I wanted to give you guys something. I found it when...well, I decided to keep looking after you left."

Michelle buried her face in her hands. "Please don't encourage them."

"I didn't find much," she added quickly. "There was nothing else in the house, but I went to Lou's storage unit and found a box with Justine's name on it. I took a picture of what was inside – I can go back and get whatever you want – but most of it was little things. Sea shells, pictures, keychain beer openers. Nothing special. But then I found this."

She reached into her bag and pulled out a black-and-white speckled notebook. "I think it was her diary. I didn't read it, but I thought you might want to have it."

Lisa reached for the soft, worn notebook and flipped to the first page. "Look, she wrote a title! 'From the Honeymoon and Beyond.'"

Val groaned. "She doodled hearts all over."

"Yeah, like hundreds of hearts," Michelle said, leaning in. She laughed. "That's so Justine."

Lisa snatched the notebook away defensively. "She was only like, twenty, when she got married. What do you expect?" Lisa looked up at Chloe. "Thanks for this. It's really nice."

She smiled. "You're welcome. I also wanted to tell you about an opportunity."

Michelle narrowed her eyes. "An opportunity?"

Chloe nodded, accepting her coffee from the waitress. "There's an Emerald conference happening tomorrow in the city. I can get you tickets, and you might be able to find more information about who Sam Beverly is."

Val clapped her hands together. "I love it. I love this plan for us."

Chloe continued. "Lou's assistant, Keith, knows everything. You just need to get him to talk."

"How do we get him to talk?" Val asked.

"Well, it won't be easy, but I've heard he's not been happy with how things are running and..."

Lisa was only half listening, instead focused on flipping through the pages of Justine's diary. At first, the entries were close together, every few days. Then the time between them stretched to months, until full years passed. Justine had filled the entire notebook, though it had taken her almost ten years.

"Awesome! I love this," Val said. "I think we can fit into her schedule. Can't we, ladies?"

"Valerie," Michelle said with a sigh. "Do you really think Lou is going to let us waltz into one of his events?"

"He probably won't see you," Chloe said. "He usually only comes for the last speech of the night. He lets the volunteers handle everything else."

"Lisa, what do you think?" Michelle asked. "Are you comfortable with this?"

"I'm not sure," she said. Her eyes drifted onto a line in the diary that was darker than the rest, as though Justine had been pressing especially hard.

Lou told me if I ever question his authority in front of the other Emeralds, he'll make sure I end up penniless and without a friend in the world. He apologized this morning, but his words are ringing in my ears.

Lisa's jaw tightened. "I think it's a great idea."

Michelle set her coffee down. "I guess I'm outvoted, then."

Thirteen

The plan was simple enough. They'd get to the conference, register for a few sessions, and find Keith. According to Chloe, Keith was unhappy with Lou, and Lou wasn't terribly happy either. Apparently, though, Lou wouldn't fire Keith, citing that he "knows where all the bodies are buried."

Val hated that phrase. It was a scummy phrase, used by scummy people who did scummy things. People like Lou Emerald.

While it would've been nice to swing by her apartment and pick up wigs for disguises, Val didn't want to risk it. Michelle and Lisa already felt sorry for her because of her divorce. She didn't want to raise questions about where all her money had gone, or have them force comments about how cozy her little dump of a place was.

They'd be fine without wigs. Lou wouldn't be there. He didn't actually attend sessions; he just showed up to collect the money at the end.

And boy did he get a lot of money. Their three "Emerald in the Rough" tickets, free of charge through Chloe, normally came in at four thousand dollars a person. Horrifyingly, that was the second cheapest package for the conference.

What a scam. Val remembered talking to Justine about the increasing prices years ago. Justine hadn't liked it. She was the one who started the sessions all those years ago, and she'd always done them for free. It all began when bright-eyed eighteen-year-old Justine had moved to Seattle. Her first job was at Lou's family's smoothie café, a place called The Emerald Escape.

The first "Emerald Polishing Session" was when Justine invited some people to come to the café after hours to talk about their lives and their goals. It grew so popular that she'd had to find bigger places to hold the events, usually at parks to get "the extra benefits of nature," as Justine put it.

Once she started dating Lou, however, everything changed. He convinced her they needed to train others so their "message" and good work could spread. He then started renting out large meeting spaces, and justified adding session fees to pay for the spaces, and to pay the trainers – though it was unclear if any of that money ever got back to them.

Justine went along with it. She wanted anyone who needed the "Emerald Way" to be able to attend. She would have preferred if it was free, but Lou said it was impossible if they wanted to reach more than ten people at a time.

She'd once told Val, her mood low and her face twisted into a frown, "Lou says it's inevitable, and as we get more popular, we need to be more exclusive. I don't know, though.

His argument is we'll be getting the people who most want to be here, but I feel like it's just the people with the most money. Or maybe the most desperation."

Lou was a master at manipulating Justine. He took her clear, pure-hearted vision and slowly chipped away at it until he had amassed what he wanted – a monstrous pile of money. Then he'd left Justine for a younger woman.

Not just one younger woman, actually. Justine discovered her marriage was over through Lou's fourth mistress. The other three had then stepped forward.

Over the years, Val had many friends, both male and female, whose partners didn't deserve them. She saw it as a spectrum, from the mildly disappointing to the truly Lifetime Movie-esque horrible partner.

Lou was the worst of all. It wasn't enough to take advantage of Justine's hard work and dedication. It wasn't enough to leave her. He took everything, absolutely everything, he could from her, and left her confused and broken.

Then, to top it off, he killed her.

● ● ●

They got to the conference hotel the next morning just before seven. It was downtown, and their anonymous arrival went smoothly except for the two blocks where a homeless man followed Lisa. He was convinced she'd made a face at him when they were crossing the street, and he threatened to "teach her a lesson."

Thankfully, his time never came, and they slipped into the lobby unscathed.

Signs directed them to the enormous front room of the conference center, with its thirty-foot ceilings and the welcome tables draped with white cloth that stretched the entire length of the room, at least fifty feet across.

The space was abuzz with excitement, and people chatted and drifted from side to side, past enormous banners of Lou's smiling face. Val stopped to glare at one particularly egregious one, his bleached white teeth the size of her hand, declaring "Emerald LA Retreat 2022: The First Stop to a New You!"

Despite the high price tag, over four hundred people were in attendance, according to the glowing red sign providing a headcount. It looked like a scoreboard.

Ugh. These poor souls just wanted to improve their lives. Who didn't?

And then there was Lou, ready to take advantage of them.

"Hi, and welcome to the Emerald Retreat," said one of the young women behind the check-in desk. "Can I have your names, please?"

"Melanie Tenderhook," Val said. "And my friends Tammy Tenderhook and Gloria Tenderhook."

Val could see Michelle putting her hands on her hips out of the corner of her eye. She expertly avoided her glare.

"Ah, perfect. I have you here. We've got a welcome bag for each of you that has everything you'll need." She reached forward to hand off three neon green cloth bags. "Have you had a chance to view the sessions online?"

Val shook her head. "Unfortunately not. This was a spur of the moment sort of thing."

"This is a sister-in-law bonding retreat for us," Lisa added rather clumsily.

She had insisted on having a backstory, and apparently thought people needed to know about it.

The woman smiled. "That's great! Is this your first time with us?"

Val spoke before Lisa could add any more backstory. "Yes."

"We are so happy you're here to grow with us. The sessions for the retreat focus on four areas of self-actualization: your cut, clarity, color, and carat! The Emerald Way teaches that by working on these four areas, you'll polish the gemstone within you and be the best version of yourself you can possibly be."

Val took a deep breath. That was a lot of gibberish to take in at once. The only person she wanted to work on cutting was Lou. Preferably with a knife, not a gemstone, but she'd take what she could get.

Michelle stepped in and covered Val's sudden silence. "That sounds wonderful. Thank you."

"Do you have any questions?"

Michelle smiled, rather skillfully feigning excitement and asking, "When will we get to meet Mr. Emerald? Is he speaking today?"

The woman's face lit up. "Of course! He'll be here for our dinner session at six o'clock. Let me see if your package includes dinner...Yes, looks like it does. You're going to love him. He is *so* inspiring."

"He seems so inspiring," Lisa said, nodding vigorously. "Just what we needed."

Val latched onto her shoulder and led her away. "Thanks again."

"Have a nice day," Michelle added, following them to a little corner of tables and chairs.

Thank goodness for Michelle. She was a far more skilled actor than Lisa, and kept a cooler head than Val. Really, they were the perfect team.

"I don't understand the whole cut and clarity thing," Lisa said once they sat down.

"Oh, you don't? Is it because it's stupid and you can't change the clarity, carat, or color of a gemstone?" Val pulled out her folder and tossed the bright green bag on the floor.

There were all kinds of trinkets in the bag – a pen, a lanyard with her fake name on it, a gaudy looking pin that looked like an emerald. All junk.

Michelle studied the packet in front of her. "It says here that clarity is your ambition as to what you want in life. Cut is your determination to go about getting it. Color is about learning to keep the fun in your life, and carat is about the worth you hold for yourself."

"Utter nonsense." Val rolled her eyes. There were too many sessions to choose from, far more than she'd expected. "Where do you think Keith will be?"

"He'll probably be running all around," Lisa said, biting a nail. "Putting out fires and the like. I don't know how we'll find him."

Val tapped the clunky green pen on her welcome packet. "I know you're not going to like this, but we should split up."

Michelle let out a sigh. "What exactly is the plan if we do find Keith? Are you just going to ask him who Sam Beverly is?"

Val shushed her. "Keep your voice down. There are ears everywhere, and hundreds of devoted Emeralds."

As if to prove her wrong, a laugh rang out from the table next to them. They looked over to see a pair of women in business suits. One of them scoffed and said, "I can't believe the C-suite is paying for us to waste our week here."

At least someone saw through this crap. Val shrugged. "All right, maybe they're not *all* devoted Emeralds, but a lot of them are."

Michelle sat back and crossed her arms. "Isn't Keith a devoted Emerald?"

"No. His loyalty has come into question, according to Chloe," Val said. That was all that Chloe knew, though. Apparently Keith didn't like her much. In general, people in the Emerald community didn't discuss their doubts about their fearless leader. If they expressed any concerns, they risked being ostracized.

Val continued. "I'm sure we'll find him. Did you both get the picture of Keith on your phone?"

Lisa and Michelle nodded.

"Good. If you find him, send a text to the group that says, 'I located the golden toilet.'"

Lisa let out a small squeal and stood, clutching her folder to her chest. "I love code words."

"Not so much the code names," Michelle said. Despite her tone, she still seemed somewhat amused.

That was good. Michelle would change her tune once they got Keith to talk.

However they managed to do that.

A bell rang out, followed by an announcement that the first session was about to start. "It's go time. I'm going to try the clarity sessions. Lisa, you do carat, and Michelle, you can do color? It's too bad we don't have a fourth person."

Michelle let out a gasp. "You're giving me color? Is that because you think I'm not fun enough?"

Val sputtered out a laugh. "I'm sorry, I didn't mean that. I'll do the color sessions."

Michelle waved a hand. "I'm just pulling your leg. I'm sure their suggestions will make me cringe and then I can justify why I don't need to be more fun."

Val didn't have time to address everything in that comment, so she just said, "Good!"

Another warning bell rang out and Lisa shot them both a panicked look. "We'll meet at lunch?"

"Yes," Val said with a nod. "Lunch."

There was no time to waste. Val took off, snagging a seat near the back of her designated banquet room. Each hour had a different focus topic, and Val sat through all four of hers.

Some of them were interesting enough, with good ideas buried deep within. The worst part was how they made them break into small groups to talk about their lives and plans. They had to brainstorm goals and barriers, write them up on glittery poster boards, then present to the large group.

Val's group was plagued by the saddest, most genuine people imaginable. One woman, desperate to change her life, had sold off her mother's engagement ring to pay for her ticket. Another man had dipped into his retirement. His wife had died three years previously and he was having a hard time finding the motivation to live.

Justine would've helped these people, so for her sake, Val tried to take the activities seriously. Her only comfort was that she hadn't sent Lisa to this group. When her backstory inevitably crumbled, she might've crumbled along with it.

Sadly, there was no sign of Keith during any of her sessions. She left a few times, pretending to make trips to the bathroom as she scanned the other rooms.

When it came time for lunch, she found Lisa and Michelle in the banquet hall. "Anything?" she asked.

"I found out I'm not very fun," Michelle said. "But you both already knew that."

"Aw, you're so fun, Shell!" Lisa hip-checked her, causing Michelle to stumble into a nearby table. She chuckled, offering Michelle a hand to steady her. "Did you have any trouble with people recognizing you, Val?"

"What?" It took Val a second to realize what she was asking. She shook her head. "No, I did not."

There seemed to be a lot of people in Emerald-brand T-shirts darting in and out of the doors in the back. If Keith would be anywhere, it was back there. The hotel staff was catering the elaborate lunch, running from table to table, getting orders and dropping off plates...

"Maybe we should go behind the scenes and poke around?" Val suggested.

Lisa put her hands on her hips. "Or maybe we should eat some of this fabulous lunch? For four grand, it has to be good."

Val let out a sigh. "Okay, fine. Quickly."

They sat at a table with five other Emerald attendees. Everyone was overly friendly, and still no one recognized her. It didn't happen often these days. Val told herself that was for the best. She liked her privacy.

In fact, it made what she was about to do a lot easier. As soon as Lisa and Michelle cleared their plates, she grabbed them each by the arm and dragged them out of their seats.

Michelle was the only one to protest. "What about dessert?"

"We'll just take a peek and then you can have your dessert." They reached the back of the hall. None of the employees paid them any attention. Everyone looked busy and stressed, talking into their earpieces and tapping away on their tablets.

A door opened, and Val slipped inside. To her annoyance, Lisa and Michelle didn't follow without prompting.

Once inside, Val pushed on. They walked through a large prep kitchen, everyone too busy to care who they were, and through a set of double doors.

"He's got to be here somewhere," Val said, turning and pushing on a swinging door labeled STAFF.

The door wouldn't budge. She resented its defiance and gave it a small kick.

It continued to defy her. She gave it a bigger kick, forcing it open with a loud thud and a groan.

Whoops.

Val rushed to the other side. "I'm so sorry, I didn't realize anyone was there and – "

She froze. It wasn't just anyone she'd nailed with the door. It was Keith, surrounded by four stern-faced men.

"What is the matter with you?" Keith barked, looking up at her and holding his head in his hand.

Lisa peeked over Val's shoulder and whispered, "I found the golden toilet."

Fourteen

"We were just looking for the bathroom," Michelle said, backing up. Lisa followed her lead, but Val stayed put.

One of the security guards knelt down to offer Keith a hand. He swatted it away as he stumbled to his feet.

Michelle's muscles tensed. Keith didn't seem like a humble, down-on-his-luck assistant. He seemed like a mini-Lou, a younger version of the tyrant.

He jerked his head toward his security team. "Get them out of here."

Michelle didn't have to be asked twice. She spun around, already through the second door, when she heard Keith speak again.

"Hang on. Aren't you Valerie Villano?"

Crap. Michelle turned to see Valerie smiling her most dazzling Hollywood smile. "I am. Are you a fan?"

He smirked. "Sure. What're you doing here?"

"We were looking for the toilet," Lisa sputtered.

Michelle shut her eyes. This was going downhill. She grabbed Val by the wrist, but she snapped her hand away.

"You're just the man I was looking for, actually. I had some questions for you."

He checked his hair in the reflection of his phone before responding. "Oh yeah? Because I've got some questions for you too." He motioned at the security guards. "Get them in a room for me. Don't forget to confiscate their phones."

The biggest of the men nodded and made a move for Valerie. She yelped and struggled, but was unable to keep hold of her purse. Lisa suffered the same fate.

A wave of panic flooded Michelle's senses. She had the absurd urge to fight them off, but after taking a step toward the security guys, she changed her mind. One of them locked eyes with her and her reaction was instantaneous.

She ran.

Michelle sprinted through the doorway and darted into the kitchen. She immediately ran into a tray of cheesecakes and knocked it to the floor, but she didn't let it slow her down.

Someone yelled out to her, yelling for her to stop. It could've been security, it could've been catering staff. She didn't know or care. She was only feet from the door, inches from freedom, and when she lunged forward, she hit a wet patch and slammed into the cold tile with a *thwack*.

That hurt. She laid there and let out a groan before slowly reaching a hand to check the shoulder she'd landed on.

A second later, a security guard heaved her up and away. Michelle tried screaming. "Help! Help me!"

He shook his head. "Yeah, yeah. You're getting bounced."

The jig was up. No one batted an eye as she disappeared through the doorway, down a deserted hall, and on to join her friends.

December 13th, 2003

*D*ear Diary,

Today is the thirteenth anniversary of the first Emerald Life Polishing Session. We just got home from an exclusive, high-level members-only banquet in Cabo to celebrate.

Everything was exquisite, just as Lou intended. I didn't see much of him because he was busy talking to donors, but his speech at the welcome dinner was beautiful. One of the volunteers put together a video of people explaining how much the Emerald Way has helped them. It made me cry. We do so much good, and I'm proud to be a part of it, even if my role is small.

I made a mistake, though. I told Lou that the new recruitment model he'd proposed made me nervous. He swears I must not be paying attention, and maybe he's right. He announced it at the event without discussing it with me beforehand, so maybe I missed something. I've been working seven days a week teaching new trainers the Emerald Way, so I've not been as present as I should be.

That's the thing, though. We're having a hard time keeping up with new sessions because we have more people who want to attend than there are trainers to teach them, but Lou is still *upset that our recruitment rate has slowed this year. It's only natural, I think, because we can only expand so fast. He disagrees. He wants to start incentivizing current Emeralds to bring in new recruits. For every new recruit they bring in, they get a cut of the new recruits' session fees.*

People are excited about it. They say it's a nice little bonus for recommendations they'd make to friends and family anyway, and it'll help them pay for their own sessions.

Here was my mistake: I told Lou it sounds a bit like a pyramid scheme.

He just about bit my head off. He hasn't talked to me in three days. I know he'll get over it eventually, and maybe he's right and I'm overreacting. It's word of mouth marketing, after all, and we can reach more people this way.

I'm just so tired. The beach was so beautiful in Cabo, but so lonely. I didn't see any animals, only a few birds, but I think the resort does something to keep them away. They're afraid of poop, I guess.

It wasn't like back home, where I could look out on the water and see a fat little harbor seal bobbing along, or an eagle, or whale fin in the distance. There's so much beauty, but it feels so empty.

- Justine

Fifteen

The three of them handled captivity differently. Val banged on the walls and called for help. Michelle paced the room, looking for exits and trying to come up with a strategy.

Lisa sat on the floor and didn't say much. From her perspective, there wasn't anything they could do. Yes, they were being held illegally, but who was there to tell? The door was locked, there were no windows or furniture, and wherever they were, no one could hear them. At least no one who cared.

On the plus side, they'd gotten their purses back. Lisa was grateful for the enormous bag she'd been dragging around with her this entire trip. She had snacks, a water bottle, and best of all, Justine's diary.

As her friends tried to deal with the reality of their situation, she slowly read through every entry in the little notebook. Some of the entries were full of hope and excitement, while others were written in a cloud of despair.

The darkness in her words was haunting. Justine admitted at one point that she turned to journaling to help her deal with negative emotions, but still. It seemed like she'd struggled far more than she let on, maintaining her funny, kind, and helpful persona.

Val eventually turned her annoyance onto Lisa. "Why are you so quiet? Aren't you angry?"

It'd been at least two hours since they'd been locked away. For Lisa, the time had flown. "What good does it do to get angry?"

Val let out a disgusted sigh before flopping onto the floor next to her. "It makes me feel a little more in control."

That was a fair point, even if it didn't make sense. "I've been reading the diary. Did you know that five years into their marriage, Justine tried to talk to Lou about starting a family?"

Michelle took a seat across from them. "What do you mean 'tried' to?"

"He wouldn't have it. Look for yourself." Lisa tossed the diary over to Michelle and watched her expression turn from a thoughtful curiosity to a deep scowl.

Michelle flipped the page and muttered, "Poor Justine."

"Let me see." Val scooted toward Michelle and read over her shoulder. Her response was less subtle. "When did he become such a monster?"

That was the question of the month, wasn't it? When they were younger, Lou seemed nice enough. He was kind to Justine. His family welcomed her like one of their own, and she was happy. She belonged. Justine had always wanted to belong.

It seemed clear to Lisa that Lou had fallen prey to a common vice: greed. Then he picked up more of the deadly sins – pride, gluttony, and a heaping of lust.

Lisa was no saint, but perhaps all those hours in Sunday school had helped her more than she realized.

She took the diary and ran her fingers over the cover. It looked a bit worn, but not as worn as it should have been. "Lou told her that if they had kids, the responsibility to raise them would be entirely hers. He said she could give up her career, but he wasn't going to do the same."

"*His* career?" Val stood again, full of fire, now shouting down at them. "He wouldn't even have a career if it weren't for Justine! He'd still be running that smoothie shop! What a pig."

Lisa laughed. "You don't even like kids."

"I don't like them for *myself*, but that doesn't mean I think other people shouldn't have them if they want. Especially someone like Justine. I just assumed she didn't want them."

"I knew she wanted kids," Michelle said softly. "After Ben died, she moved in with me to help with Tyler. She kept joking she was going to become his adoptive second mother."

Lisa sat up, her hip popping as she did. "You never told me this."

Michelle looked up at her, a sad smile on her face. "I know. I was ashamed. After Ben died, I had a hard time getting out of bed. I couldn't do basic things like get groceries. Justine moved in for three months until I was able to function again. She never told you?"

Lisa and Val shook their heads. "Never."

"That's Justine." Michelle paused. "She would've been a great mom."

"Just when I thought I couldn't get more angry for Justine..." Val let out a small scream and kicked her high heel into the wall. It left no mark.

She let out a huff. "When we get out of here, I'm going to double my efforts to prove you-know-who did you-know-what."

Lisa narrowed her eyes. "You mean – "

Val cut her off. "Don't say it. They could be listening."

"It doesn't matter," Michelle said. "I don't think we're getting out of here alive. They'll tell everyone that we became Emerald Elites and that we've disappeared to run this circus."

Val nodded. "Yeah, that tracks."

Yeesh. Lisa didn't realize her friends were *that* defeated. She reclaimed her seat against the wall. "They're just trying to scare us. We haven't done anything wrong."

"Since when are you so cool under pressure?" Val asked.

She shrugged. "This isn't real trouble. I know what getting in trouble feels like, and this isn't it."

They both looked at her questioningly, and she almost spilled the beans about Neil.

Almost.

Instead, she started reading aloud from Justine's diary. After one entry, she passed it to Val, who gave a much livelier reading, complete with a deep, boorish voice for Lou.

Before long, both Michelle and Val were too enthralled by the ghosts of Justine's words to worry about being trapped in an empty, windowless room.

They were nearly through the entire thing when they heard someone approaching.

They stood expectantly, and the door opened to reveal the smug face of their captor, Keith.

"Hello, ladies," he said as two of the large security guards filed in on either side of him.

He was too afraid to face three little women by himself? Coward.

"We'd like to leave," Michelle said firmly. "Or we'll be pressing charges."

Keith laughed. "You signed up to be here all week. Do you think the police are really going to believe your sob story?"

"All *week*!" Val spat the words out and got closer to him. "We didn't sign up to be locked in a box for a week."

He shrugged. "I guess you had a misunderstanding."

"You can't keep us here," Michelle insisted. "It's illegal."

He smiled the confident, easy smile of someone who believed consequences were only for others. "And it was illegal when you broke into Lou's homes."

Val took a step back.

"Oh, you thought we didn't know? Talk about breaking the law. Tsk tsk." He wagged a finger at Val.

She narrowed her eyes. "We were guests."

"Yes, right, of Chloe. Lou is taking care of her, too."

Val turned around, her big eyes stretched, and mouthed, "*Taking care of her!*"

Michelle shook her head and took a step closer. "I would love to talk to Lou. Where is he?"

One of the security guards stepped between them, bumping Michelle with his shoulder and knocking her off balance.

Lisa had seen enough. This whole thing was ridiculous. Real police didn't act like this. They weren't allowed to. Lisa had first-hand knowledge of how real police questioned people, because she had been questioned before she was fired.

She walked up to the security guards and said, "Excuse me. I need to use the ladies' room."

The two of them looked at each other, puzzled, then back at Keith.

He shook his head. "Lou's going to make time in his schedule to deal with you three." With that, he turned and walked out the door, locking it behind him.

Michelle turned to Val. "Is it me, or does he seem like a guy who's still loyal to Lou?"

"I don't know," Val said, exasperated. "Or does he just enjoy a power trip?"

Lisa let out a sigh. "Oh yes. Looks like a power trip to me."

Michelle spoke again, her voice low, her tone cautious. "Did Chloe set us up? What if it was wrong to trust her? Maybe she's just as big of an Emerald as the rest of them."

"Definitely not." Val stopped her pacing to look at them. "He made it sound like Lou killed her, don't you think? 'Took care of her?'"

Michelle shook her head. "No. He didn't kill her. They probably pulled this off together."

"That doesn't make any sense. She's a nice girl caught in a bad situation." Val straightened her posture. "Honestly, if she was on Lou's side, she could've had us arrested red-handed at the cliff house."

Michelle frowned. "That's a good point. What are we going to do if he decides to keep us for a week?"

Lisa listened to them going back and forth without saying a word. They couldn't keep them in this room forever. The week-long thing was a bluff, probably to keep them from calling the police the first chance they had. As was the break-in accusation.

It was all a Lou game, like the ones he'd played on Justine for years. That was what the diary documented – years and years of Lou putting Justine down, making her question herself, and keeping her afraid.

Lisa, however, wasn't blinded by years of Lou's alternating love and abuse. She wasn't going to let him win.

●●●

When Lou finally arrived, Michelle and Val were ready. Not for the extra security he brought – a grand total of six guys – but they were ready to yell at him.

As soon as the door opened, they started shouting, finger pointing, and telling him how badly he was going to pay.

He watched them, a solemn look on his face and waited until they were done. Finally, he spoke. "Ladies, I consider you all friends. Why so much anger?"

"You're going to let us out of this room," Val said.

He looked over his shoulder at Keith. "There must have been some kind of misunderstanding. Of course you can leave. You've been free to leave this entire time."

Michelle crossed her arms. "Right."

A smile curled his lips. "I'm so curious what got you interested in coming to my home, then to my conference. I just can't figure it out."

Lisa stepped out from behind her friends. Her voice was even and quiet, her stance non-threatening. "It was all because of a friend of ours."

He smiled down at her. "Justine?"

She shook her head.

"Ah, someone new." He let out a chuckle. "It's nice you can still make friends at your age."

Lisa nodded. "Yes. His name is Sam Beverly. Do you know him?"

He stared at her, lips still pulled into a wide smile over his bright porcelain veneers. "Oh?"

She took a step toward him and lightly pushed him in the shoulder.

The security guards moved toward her, but he quickly threw a hand up, motioning for them to stand back.

Lisa smiled at him. "We'd like our phones back, please."

"Give them back," Lou said to Keith.

Keith was bewildered. "But – "

"*Now!*"

He produced their phones and, without another word, the three of them filed past.

Sixteen

They burst out of the room, Lisa leading the way to a clearly marked exit door. They went straight for it, pushing it open and spilling onto the sidewalk, the stuffy night air filling their lungs.

"Freedom!" Val yelled. She looked over her shoulder to make sure they weren't being followed. It looked clear. "Let's find a place with people. Witnesses, so we're protected."

"There's a coffee shop over there," Michelle said, pointing.

Val nodded. "That'll do."

"Good idea," Lisa said.

When they got there, Lisa disappeared into the bathroom. Val waited to confront Lisa until after she emerged. "Okay, where on *earth* did that come from?"

She shrugged. "I've had to go for the last two hours."

Val laughed and shook her head. "Not that. I mean you standing up to Lou. Who *are* you?"

"I'm just little old me!" She walked over to the counter and peered at the menu on the wall. "Did you guys order anything yet? I'm thirsty."

Michelle shot Val an alarmed look and lowered her voice. "Did they do something to her in there? Inject her with something?"

Lisa spun around. "I don't know why you're acting so strange about this. Clearly, the longer they kept us there, the more trouble they were in. They brought Lou in as a final act to scare us. It didn't work."

"But..." Val trailed off, staring at Lisa. She didn't know what to think, or what to say.

A man appeared behind them. "Are you in line?"

Val said "no" at the same time Lisa said "yes."

"I'm thirsty after all that," she said.

They ordered drinks and took a seat at a booth facing the window. Val wanted to be sure they could see anyone who might be coming after them.

Michelle kept a close watch, too. Her nerves seemed just as shot as Val's. "Should we call the police and report them?"

"I don't know." Val sat back, relishing the cushy booth. It felt nice to not be sitting on the floor. "He could just come after us and claim we'd broken into his vacation homes."

"That's true." Michelle frowned.

Val turned to Lisa. "What do you think?"

Lisa looked up from her phone. "What? I'm sorry. Did I miss something?"

Val leaned in. "Is Lou sending you threatening texts or something?"

She forced a smile. "No. It's Neil. He's...I don't know. He left me four voicemails."

"Is he okay?" asked Michelle.

Lisa took a long sip of her iced green tea. "Not really."

Uh oh. Val suddenly remembered Chloe might be in trouble, too. She pulled out her phone, relieved to see a text from her dancing on the screen. The preview said, "Lou dumped me. He was pretty mad, but I asked him about..."

She'd read the rest later. At least Chloe was alive.

"What's wrong?" Val asked. "Do you need to go home?"

"No." Lisa let out a sigh. "I don't know. Maybe. He called and said there's no food in the house, he doesn't have any money, and...it's just a mess. He's gambling again."

"Oh." Val sunk into her seat. "I'm sorry."

"It's okay. It's not your fault. It's not anyone's fault. He's just..." She shrugged.

Val felt so sorry for her. Neil had always been pathetic, not malignant like Lou. Yeah, he was sort of a bum, but it seemed to work for them. Lisa was her same, bubbly self, and she never complained. He didn't deserve Lisa, but she'd always seemed happy, so Val didn't question it.

But now she looked tired. So very tired.

"If you need to go home, we understand," Michelle said.

Val nodded. "Yeah, of course. We appreciate you, and you were the real MVP back there, but if Neil needs you..." Her voice trailed off. She didn't actually want Lisa to leave, but what was she going to do? Tell her to abandon her husband?

Lisa nodded, eyes down. "I don't want to talk about all of that. This trip has been such a wonderful break from his problems." She looked up. "It's rare I get a break from his problems."

Wow, that was bleak. Val didn't know what to say, so she just sat there, hoping Lisa felt the solidarity in her silence.

After a moment, Lisa spoke again. "Reading all of those entries from Justine's diary made me feel...I don't know. Something. I'm angry for her. I'm angry Lou didn't love her the way she deserved to be loved."

Michelle nodded, her eyes misty. "Justine was a gift to this world."

Val bit her lip. Her vision was getting cloudy, too, but she didn't want to face any of that sadness. She didn't want to think about her sweet friends' terrible marriages, or her own terrible marriage, or any of it.

Her thoughts drifted to Lou and sharpened. Anger trumped sadness, pushed it aside and allowed her to breathe.

"Something is clearly up with Lou," Val finally said. "You saw his face when you said Sam's name. He folded like a house of cards. We're going to figure it out. For Justine."

"Yeah." Lisa nodded. "I'm not going home. Not yet. Neil is an adult; he can figure it out for a few more days. I want to go back to Venice Beach."

"Oh?"

She dabbed at her nose with a stiff paper napkin. There was a smile on her face now. "I think we should spread Justine's ashes there. After that, we can find Mr. Beverly."

Michelle reached across and grabbed her hand. "Let's do it."

Val smiled. It had taken long enough, but they were finally all in.

Seventeen

The dreaded announcement rang overhead. It was time to switch to airplane mode and stow carry-ons.

It was time for takeoff.

How did the flight attendant's voice always sound so calm and collected? Michelle pulled her phone from her purse and saw a message from Arthur. "Good luck on your flight. Looks like clear skies all the way to Maine!"

That was nice. Of course, he could be lying to make her feel better. And planes could crash during nice weather. Mechanical issues didn't care about the weather.

She thanked him anyway and clicked into airplane mode.

The plane rolled down the runway and Michelle gritted her teeth. She shot a look at her friends – all smiles, deep in conversation about Sam Beverly.

She couldn't deal with that right now. Maybe it was time for Val's takeoff care package? She'd resisted using it, but with how her heart was pounding in her chest, she figured it couldn't hurt.

Michelle opened the little heart-covered bag and pulled out a pair of noise canceling headphones. She slipped them on, plugged in her phone, and pulled up the relaxing playlist she'd downloaded earlier. Then she pulled the mask over her eyes and tried to sit back and relax.

Val must've infused it with perfume. It was a pleasant, flowery sort of scent, disguising the smell of stale coffee and ozone in the cabin. It reminded her of the massage she'd gotten in Miami...

The noise canceling function of the headphones was surprisingly effective. She didn't know how it worked, but wow. What a difference. She could *almost* pretend she wasn't in a giant metal tube, forty thousand feet in the air, propelled by turbines and explosions.

The first song began, edging in with soft synthesizer tones and a delicate piano concerto. It faded with the sound of a stream and raindrops.

That got her through the sensation of takeoff. She was tempted to peek out and see if the plane engines were still attached, or if they were on fire, but she decided against it.

The next song was a violin blended with the sound of crashing waves. Then a forest with twittering birds. And on and on...

She made it nearly two hours into the flight before she removed the headphones and took off the mask.

When she opened her eyes, Val was beaming at her, a Bloody Mary in each hand. "Perfect timing! I was hoping to share one of these with you. I mean, I can obviously handle them on my own, but my *intent* was to share with you."

"Thanks." Michelle accepted the tall glass, carefully balancing the set of skewers on top. One was packed with olives, squares of cheese, tiny pickles, and tomatoes. The second skewer was more adventurous – a small grilled cheese sandwich, a soft pretzel bite, and a mini pizza bagel.

Val smiled. "Cheers!"

Michelle nodded and returned her smile before looking outside. Everything seemed fine. All she could see were white clouds, and the flight attendants weren't panicking. That was always a good sign.

"Did I miss anything?" she asked.

Lisa leaned in from across the aisle. "I had a brilliant idea. I paid for Wi-Fi and requested the medical examiner's report for Justine's death."

"Oh, lovely." Michelle pretended like that was a totally normal thing to do and took a sip of her drink.

It burned, forcing her into a cough. She'd forgotten to mix the vodka that had pooled at the bottom. First class sure did make their drinks strong. "Did they answer you?"

"Not yet," Lisa said. "Hopefully soon."

Michelle took a bite of the grilled cheese. It was cold, but still tasty. Next, she took a bite of the pizza. Also surprisingly good.

She mixed the drink using the slice of bacon sticking out of her glass and took another sip.

Much better. All the salt would have her bloated like a balloon by the end of the flight, but she didn't care. For the moment she wasn't afraid of dying, and that made the inevitable fluid retention worthwhile.

"I talked to Chloe before we took off," Val said. "She said Lou threatened her before he broke up with her."

Michelle raised an eyebrow. "What did he say?"

"You know, the usual. That she'd go nowhere in life, and she was banned from ever attending an Emerald meeting again. Blah blah, who cares. You know she already contacted her PhD program and they said they'd be happy to take her back?"

"That's great." Michelle's quiet paranoia that Chloe had set them up finally faded. Michelle's default state was to be suspicious until proven otherwise, but it didn't make sense.

Lou had outed Chloe as innocent. He had also revealed that Keith had no idea who Sam Beverly was, which did make things a bit more mysterious.

"Are you feeling okay?" Lisa asked.

Michelle nodded. "Yeah, I think so. Better than before."

"With your low alcohol tolerance, you're only two Bloody Marys away from a really good nap," Val said with a laugh.

"Did you slip a Benadryl in one of these olives?" Michelle asked, pulling away and staring at the glass.

Val snapped her fingers. "Shoot, no. That would've been smart."

Michelle was able to focus on reading a book for the remainder of the flight. They then had a smooth, quick landing and a two-hour layover in Boston before their short hour-and-twenty-minute flight to Maine.

As they got ready to board, Michelle caught sight of the plane in the window. It was a puny little thing, not like the massive Boeings she'd gotten used to. That meant no first class, no emergency safety slides, no anything, really, didn't it?

Maybe they got parachutes? Michelle had watched these small planes fly around San Juan Island for years and was never tempted to get in one. They ended up in the ocean too frequently for her tastes. Arthur assured her it wasn't a common occurrence, but she couldn't be convinced.

Now here she was, walking on board like a fool.

She told herself it was for Justine, because it was. The answers they needed, if they existed, were in Maine.

Despite being in a much smaller and jumpier metal tube, the flight went quickly. Michelle was now used to five-hour flights, apparently. This was nothing, and she hardly had time to worry about landing before it was announced they were touching down.

It was a relief when they landed at the little community airport. It was only a two-mile drive to Mount Desert Island.

Zora had arranged for a rental car to be waiting for them at the airport, and the keys were at the front desk. She was incredible, and the last piece of their journey seemed within reach. Michelle suddenly felt the full weight of the excitement, the feeling that had been held back by her flying anxiety.

They piled into the car and Lisa drove them right onto Mount Desert Island.

How odd it was to drive to an island. Michelle was glad there were no roads to San Juan, despite how convenient it might make things. She liked being remote.

Yet the ease of this journey was unquestionable. Within minutes, they were on the island and only a few miles from the town of Bar Harbor, where they were staying, and from Acadia National Park.

Michelle couldn't wait to see it. There were an incredible number of hikes and magnificent views ahead of them. This was the part of the trip she'd been waiting for.

Lisa drove on slowly, and Val remarked how much the route reminded her of San Juan. They rode past alternating tall forests, farms, and spread out two-story homes. Every now and then they saw a sign for a bakery, or an ice cream shop, or a lobster shack.

It was calm. Nice.

Michelle was glad she'd made it. This was her pace, much more than Los Angeles or Miami.

The only thing they were missing were views of the sea. That was soon corrected as they got nearer to town. The houses grew closer together and glimpses of the water appeared behind the trees.

They hit town and Michelle's chest tightened. It was adorable, like something from a magazine. They passed a little inn with ivy growing up the side, then a slew of shops, all cheerful yellows or blues or bright, clean whites.

Despite being thousands of miles from Friday Harbor, Bar Harbor had captured the same coastal charm. It looked like a little fishing village, albeit with some upgrades for tourists to enjoy.

After much oohing, aahing and pointing, they pulled away from town and onto a quiet street. The GPS announced they'd arrived just as they hit the opening of a deserted-looking gravel road.

Lisa stopped the car. She already drove with her chin almost at the steering wheel, but she leaned even further forward to peer ahead. "I can't see anything past all of these trees. Do you think the house is down there?"

"Must be," Michelle said.

Lisa let out a sigh and settled back into her regular driving position. "Let's see."

They traveled slowly on the gravel, bumping and rocking their way until a white and green farmhouse appeared amidst the trees.

"That's it," Val said, pointing. "I recognize it from the pictures."

Lisa parked and they all got out. They could hear nothing but the wind whispering through the trees and the twinkling of a wind chime on the porch.

"It's adorable," Michelle said quietly.

"It is." Val said.

The three of them stood there for a moment and stared.

Val was the first to move toward the door, and Michelle followed. As soon as they walked in, they were greeted by the delicate smell of fresh cut flowers. The inside of the house was all rich hardwoods and simple white walls.

Near the staircase, there was a large print showing various nautical knots. Another large portrait showed a sunset in Friday Harbor with a ferry moseying in to dock. Michelle walked on, admiring the paintings and pictures of mountains, whales, and harbor seals.

She smiled. Justine had made this place her own. She'd transformed this little house into a beautifully updated cottage fit for a modern-day business woman. One who was, perhaps, a tad homesick.

Lisa squealed from behind her. "I just got an email back from the medical examiner!"

Val rushed over. "Open it!"

Lisa dropped her phone when Val appeared behind her. "Don't scare me like that!"

"I'm sorry! I'm excited."

Michelle stepped closer. Her throat felt dry. This could be the answer they'd been waiting for, the one that would put their theories to rest.

Lisa jabbed at her phone with her finger like a crow pecking at spilled popcorn. She let out a groan. "They said the report won't be available for four to eight weeks, and then it will only be available to next of kin."

Ah, of course. That would have been too easy. Michelle took a seat at the bottom of the staircase. "I guess that's that."

Val shook her head. "We'll have Tammy request it."

"But what if it takes eight weeks?" Lisa let out a sigh.

A smile crossed Val's lips. "We still have Sam Beverly."

Eighteen

It didn't take long for them to get comfortable in the house. It was much cozier than the other homes Justine and Lou had bought together, and while it wasn't as luxurious as a hotel, it just felt right.

Lisa dropped her bag off in one of the upstairs bedrooms before going downstairs, through the back door, and out to the edge of the property to stare at the ocean. It was mesmerizing – the soft sound of the water lapping the shore, a boat puttering away in the distance, a pair of birds calling overhead.

It was like she'd been pulled out of a week-long party and plunged into a secret garden. The quiet was like a blanket, covering everything from Neil's nagging voicemails to her echoing thoughts of their now-empty bank account.

Lisa was halfway down the stairs to the dock below when Michelle emerged from the house and insisted she come inside.

"*Come on!* Change into some comfortable clothes. We're going into town."

Lisa shot her a pleading look, but she got nothing in return. Michelle's face was set in a stern stare. Her newfound energy was frightening. Perhaps her recent near-death experience with flying on a Cessna had gotten to her?

"I'm serious." Michelle turned toward the house, then stopped, returning to face Lisa. "What's the point of having a house so close to town if we don't even get to walk around?"

"Okay, okay!" Lisa put her hands up. "I'll get changed. I can drive."

"No, let's walk. It's so close! And so pretty."

Lisa's hips were stiff from being stuck on the floor the day before. Walking wasn't appealing in the least. "Why can't we drive?"

Michelle shook her head before turning and walking off. "We'd have to fight over parking."

Lisa followed her inside and watched as she ordered Val upstairs to change into "hiking or walking-appropriate clothes."

Val didn't protest, instead diving into the suitcase she'd left on the living room floor. "What if I didn't bring walking clothes, exactly?"

"What!" Michelle stared down at her from the midway point of the stairs. She was ready, dressed in a short-sleeved moisture wicking shirt, heavily pocketed shorts, and hiking boots.

Lisa suppressed a smile. Apparently, this was the moment Michelle had been waiting for.

"I didn't have room," Val whined. "I needed to fit all the stuff for Miami and LA."

Michelle crossed her arms. "Do you at least have sneakers?"

Val nodded. "Yes ma'am."

"I can loan you clothes, then, and we can wash them before our hike tomorrow."

"I'll just save that for tomorrow," Val said, making a face only Lisa could see.

Michelle shrugged. "Suit yourself."

Lisa rushed up the stairs. Her small suitcase hadn't allowed for much, and she needed to run a load of laundry, but she at least had her gym shoes and a few pairs of shorts. That would have to do for now.

When she returned, Val was half-dressed and arguing with Michelle.

"It's on the itinerary," Michelle said, holding up a sheet.

"A hike *and* a bike ride? Doesn't that seem like a lot?"

"We've been sitting around eating and drinking for days! Doesn't it seem overdue?"

Val shook her head and plunged into her bag. "No, not really."

"There's a national park just down the street," Michelle said. "We are not going to miss out on it. Zora marked a bunch of Justine's favorite hikes. We have to at least try some."

Val emerged, gripping a handful of shirts in her fist. "Fine. I'll do a hike. But just one."

"Where's the bike ride?" asked Lisa. "Along the shore? That'd be nice."

Michelle shook her head, eyes filling with glee. "No, we're going to bike on the carriage roads in Acadia. John Rockefeller built them so people could enjoy 'motor free travel.' You can bike, ride horses – "

Lisa interrupted her. "Oh! I love horses!"

"No," Val said firmly. "No horses. I don't trust anything with a mind of its own."

"Sorry, Lisa," Michelle said before turning back to Val. "The trails can get hilly, though, so we should probably rent e-bikes. They have a motor to assist up hills."

Val scoffed, lacing up a pair of perfectly white sneakers. "Again, no thanks with the mind of its own thing."

Michelle crossed her arms. "It has no more mind of its own than a car does."

"What's the point of going on a bike ride if you don't get any exercise out of it?" Val stood, pulling on a shirt from the pile. "I'm going to be renting a traditional, non-motorized bike."

Lisa made herself look away. She hadn't meant to stare, but Val had kept herself in such great shape. Maybe she should follow her lead and rent a regular, non-motorized bike, too?

"You'll still get plenty of exercise," Michelle mumbled under her breath.

"I don't want to coast along the whole time."

Lisa watched helplessly as they shot barbs back and forth. It was a classic argument. Both people knew they were right, so naturally, they got nowhere except on each other's nerves.

The bickering continued during their walk to town. It was just under a mile, and Val seamlessly transitioned to arguing for her requirements of an acceptable hike.

"Ideally no hills, because then – "

"No hills!" Michelle stopped dead in her tracks, turning around. "You can't get any views if you're afraid of walking up a hill!"

Lisa kept out of it. As much as she'd dreaded walking, her hips were starting to loosen and feel better. The sun was shining. Birds were singing. It was a marvelous day.

They reached town, and it was so adorable it almost hurt. Even Val and Michelle's war was silenced as they skirted the sidewalks, joining the other bunches of tourists who were passing the cute little shops and restaurants.

They popped inside the shops one by one as their interests were piqued. Lisa got lobster claw bottle openers for the kids. Michelle bought a map of the carriage roads from a hiking shop. Val swooned over paintings in an art gallery, finally settling on buying herself a small, coin-sized carving of a sailboat.

At the center of town, there was a large green space and a fountain flanked by flowers. They asked a woman to take their picture there, just the three of them, smiling in front of the fountain.

They walked on, pulled by the charms of the restaurants and beer gardens. People were sitting outside, laughing and enjoying a well-earned beer after obviously muddy hikes. There were dogs, too, wagging their tails, mouths open in the heat, relaxing on the restaurant patios next to their owners.

No wonder Michelle had changed into her best hiking gear. She fit right in. Even Lisa, in her more touristy getup, managed to blend in. For the first time, it was Val who was out of place in her pleather pants and tight white button down.

They stopped in for a bite to eat at a café, opting for a table outside.

"All right, what's our plan to find Sam?" Val asked.

Lisa closed her eyes and sat back. The weather was so perfect, and the mood was much more relaxed than the other places they'd visited. She didn't feel the pressure to have fun. She was already having fun.

"I thought you had a plan," Michelle said.

Val shook her head. "Not really. Maybe we can find a phone book?"

"A phone book?" Michelle repeated. "That's your brilliant idea? Just look up every Beverly in the area and say 'Hey, did you happen to threaten Lou Emerald?'"

"What if Sam doesn't live here and was only here on vacation?" Lisa mused.

The thought had been nagging her ever since they'd found out about the email. The blank stares she received in return made her realize no one else had thought of this.

"I don't know." Val drummed her nails on the table. "Why don't we just email him and say...hi?"

"You think 'hi' is going to do it?" Michelle dropped her menu to the table with a flop. "What if he doesn't use that email anymore? What if it was just for blackmail?"

Lisa bit her lip. "She might be right. Why would he use his regular email to commit a crime?"

Val released an exasperated sigh, soliciting looks from the table next to them. "Then what are we supposed to do? We can't get the medical examiner's report, we can't find Sam, and Lou certainly isn't going to talk. We're stuck."

She lunged into her purse and pulled out a package of Tic Tacs, struggling with the top for a moment before forcefully throwing it at the table.

"Okay," Lisa said slowly, reaching for the Tic Tacs. "I didn't know you were so upset. We'll figure it out."

"I'm not so sure, Lisa." Val put her sunglasses on and looked away. "If you haven't noticed, things haven't gone very well for us recently."

Michelle giggled, and Lisa shot her a look.

Luckily, Val didn't get angrier. She just slumped down in her chair.

Poor Val. Lisa popped the Tic Tacs open and handed them back to her. "We will figure it out. Maybe not by the end of this trip, but eventually. I'm sure of it."

"Are you?" She shook her head, stuffing a handful of orange Tic Tacs into her mouth. "Because it seems pretty hopeless to me."

Michelle looked up from her hiking book. "We can ask around for Sam. Look him up on Facebook, maybe?"

"Look him up on Facebook?" Val let out a sigh. "Why do we even bother? Why not rent a plane and have them pull a banner with his name on it?"

"I bet Avery could find him," Lisa said.

Val turned to her. "Is he good with computers?"

She shrugged. "Yes, I think so. I don't know if he could find someone with just their email, but I can ask?"

"Why didn't you mention this before?" The excitement in Val's voice was growing.

Lisa was glad to see Val's mood turning. Her panic always grew with other people's discontent. "I don't know. I thought you knew where he was already." She laughed. "I half expected him to be waiting at the house on your order!"

Val clapped her hands together. "This is great! Can you call Avery now?"

"Sure."

Michelle cleared her throat. "Okay. After that, can we please agree which hikes we're willing to do?"

Lisa smiled. Everyone had their priorities. She was happy as long as everyone else was happy. "Of course."

Nineteen

There was a strange calm to Justine's cottage that made it hard for Val to fall asleep. It was too private and far too quiet. It'd be easy for someone to sneak in and kill them all. No one would know, and they couldn't call for help. Their phones never seemed to have service, and the next neighbor was too far away to hear.

To calm her nerves, Val opened the bedroom windows and let the sound of summer bugs pour in. It also allowed her to listen for incoming attacks.

The most treacherous thing she discovered was a pair of deer that noisily stepped on some leaves near the house. Before catching sight of them, she had convinced herself the end was near.

Eventually, she managed to fall asleep, and when she woke, she could just make out the sound of water gently brushing up to the shore.

They'd survived the night. That was good.

The room was too cold, though. She got out of bed and shut the window, spotting the hiking outfit Michelle had laid out for her.

Oh, Michelle. She'd argue it was perfect weather to hike, that it was their duty to Justine, and something about the Vanderbilts, but Val didn't want to hike. She wanted to know what had happened to Justine.

For the first time, she wasn't sure they would ever find out. They'd run out of ideas and run out of leads. Val felt hopeless. What was next? One of them would die unexpectedly, too?

Fate made no promises. Life could end in an instant. Dead, with no warning. Cold. Gone.

A shiver ran down her back. She needed to get dressed, and she didn't feel like arguing anymore with Michelle. At least the clothes were comfortable.

Once ready, Val made her way down to the kitchen. She'd hoped to be the first one up, but Michelle was already there, wide awake and ready to rumble.

"Oh good! I've been waiting for someone else to get up. Now I'm allowed to start making noise."

Val yawned. "What time is it?"

"7:34." Michelle didn't miss a beat. "You look nice."

"Thanks."

"I was thinking I could throw together a quick breakfast, put some coffee into mugs, and we could get going?"

Val took a seat at the kitchen island. "Do we have to go this early? Maybe we should relax, stroll back into town, talk to some of the locals?"

"Well..." Michelle glanced at the pan heating up on the stove. "I guess we could do that. But this hike is exceptionally beautiful and popular. I'm afraid if we wait until later, the parking lot may fill up and we won't be able to – "

Val held up a hand. "Okay. We'll go now."

Lisa emerged from her bedroom just as Michelle doled out scrambled eggs, bacon, and toast. They ate, Lisa changed into her loaned hiking clothes, and they piled into the car for the short drive to Acadia National Park.

They'd agreed to do the Ocean Path Trail near the southern tip of the island. It started at Sand Beach, which Val liked the sound of, and went just over two miles.

Or so she'd thought. When Val initially agreed to the hike, she didn't realize that it was two miles *each way*.

There was no point in complaining. Val dutifully followed along, clutching her wide-brimmed hat whenever they neared the water and the wind threatened to blow it away.

They hiked along the hillside with the rocky coast always within view. At times, they had to scramble onto the pink granite shores, carefully avoiding getting their shoes stuck in the crevices.

It wasn't the type of beach she preferred, but it was still breathtaking, and they all stood in awe as the waves crashed in.

When they finally got back to the car, Val saw she had a message from Zora. "Let me know if the itinerary isn't to your liking, or if you aren't enjoying the restaurant choices. I'm happy to adjust!"

Val read the message aloud. "Zora's on top of everything. Do you think she knows more about Justine's death?"

"I've been wondering the same thing," Michelle said.

"You mean," Val dropped her voice, "she could be a suspect?"

"What?" Michelle flashed her annoyed look. "No, I don't think she's a suspect. I don't think anyone hurt – "

Lisa cut her off. "Zora's not a suspect! The poor woman was barely holding it together when we met with her on San Juan."

Michelle nodded. "Right."

Lisa continued. "Don't you think if she knew something, she would've told the police?"

"Ugh. Yeah, you're right." Val let out a sigh. "What if she knows Sam Beverly? It wouldn't hurt to ask."

Michelle and Lisa disagreed with her, but she decided to ask anyway. She wrote a message back. "Everything has been perfect! We're having so much fun. Thank you, Zora. Out of curiosity, do you know someone named Sam Beverly?"

Zora started writing back immediately. Val stared at the three bouncing dots on her phone's screen as Lisa and Michelle chatted in the front seat.

"Glad you're having fun! No, can't say that I do. Sorry!"

Oh well. Just another dead end.

They picked up lobster rolls and French fries before going back to the house to rest. Michelle wanted to go on another hike, but neither Val nor Lisa were up for it. They convinced her to spend another evening on the town, and when they were out at dinner, Lisa got a call from her son.

"Hello?" she answered, her tone bright.

Val zeroed in on Lisa, trying to pick up on any subtle facial expressions or clues as to what Avery was saying.

"Oh really?" Lisa smiled. "That's great! How'd you do that? *Oh.*" She nodded and threw a thumbs up at Val. "That's incredible. You're so good with these things."

Lisa continued talking to Avery for another agonizing ten minutes.

When she finally hung up, Val asked, "What did he say?"

"He found Sam!"

Val let out a squeal. "Is he local?"

Lisa nodded. "He works at a seafood place nearby. Avery said he was really easy to find. He just searched for him online along with the word 'Acadia.' Sam's picture was on the restaurant's Facebook page."

"Let's go!" Val said, standing up.

Lisa shook her head. "It's already closed for the day. But we can go tomorrow."

Michelle frowned. "What about our bike ride?"

"We can go on a bike ride some other time," Val said. "What time does this place open?"

Lisa squinted at her phone. "Looks like eleven."

Michelle sat back and let out a sigh. "We could have our whole bike ride done before eleven."

Val stared at her. They wouldn't have any peace until Michelle got to ride that stupid motorized bicycle. "Fine. But we need to be at that restaurant the moment it opens."

"Fine."

"Fine," Lisa added, her tone light. "If you're forcing me to have lobster for lunch again tomorrow, then that is my cross to bear."

Twenty

The bike rental place didn't open until eight in the morning. Michelle would've picked the bikes up the night before if she'd known.

"This isn't a good start to our day," she announced after the bicycle shop employee disappeared into a back room.

"There's still plenty of day left," Lisa said.

It took almost half an hour to complete the rental forms and get sized for their bikes. Michelle managed to convince Lisa to rent an e-bike with forty-five miles of range, but Val refused to budge.

"We're only doing eight miles. How bad can it be?"

While Michelle and Lisa practiced turning their motors on and off, Val made a short trip to the car to dump her helmet. "I don't need this messing up my hair."

Michelle was tired of arguing with her. If she wanted to exhaust herself and sustain a head injury, that was her right.

Once Lisa said she felt comfortable enough to start, Michelle started out on the trail. For the first time in hours, she couldn't hear Val's voice. It was marvelously peaceful, and riding through the twists and turns of the forest was nothing short of magnificent.

The trail was wide and the edges were lined with enormous slabs of granite. Michelle had read that this was engineered by John Rockefeller, and he'd taken the landscape of the island into consideration when planning the carriage roads. How lovely that everyone could now enjoy this masterpiece, and not just the rich?

Only Val seemed to be untouched by this. Probably because she was rich and used to luxury. She'd said as much, even.

They started up the first hill and climbed steadily for nearly a mile. Both Michelle and Lisa started getting winded after a few minutes and kicked their motors on. It was a nice break, and they reached the top of the hill with ease.

As they waited for Val to catch up, Michelle couldn't help herself. "I guess Val's not in as in as good of shape as she thought she was..."

"Be nice," Lisa warned, voice low. "I think she's tired. I don't think she's been sleeping well."

"Why not?"

"It's too quiet for her, I guess. Plus she's afraid that Lou will come back and finish the job with the three of us."

Michelle rolled her eyes. Val was such a drama queen. "I highly doubt that."

Yes, Michelle agreed there was something off about Lou, but Justine hadn't sent them on this trip to waste all of their time thinking about him. Maybe there was something off about Justine's death, too, but Michelle still didn't believe their friend had been murdered.

It would've been nice to get the coroner's report. It was the only thing that could put Val's fears to rest.

Michelle was trying to be understanding of Val. It seemed like Val couldn't get over how *she* felt about Justine's death. Yes, Justine's death felt wrong because it *was* wrong. Justine had been a beautiful soul, full of life and love.

Val was in denial, but there was no need to push her over the edge now.

After a few minutes, Val appeared, slowly pumping her legs and inching her bicycle up the hill. "I did it!" she announced when she stopped next to them, breathless and red-cheeked.

Michelle nodded. "We've got a downhill coming up here, and then we've got a real climb. I hope you're ready."

"All I do is get ready," Val said flatly.

Michelle ignored her comment and kicked off, enjoying the thrill as her bike picked up speed. Lisa rode alongside her, a grimace on her face. "We're going too fast!" she yelled, hitting the brakes and slowing down considerably.

Michelle didn't slow down. She leaned forward, picking up more speed. It felt like she was flying through the trees. It was freeing.

The downhills always went so much more quickly than the uphills, and they reconvened where the trail leveled out.

Val's mood seemed to have improved. "That was really fun."

Michelle smiled. "See? I told you you'd like it."

"This next hill doesn't look too bad," Lisa said.

Michelle pulled out her map and counted the elevation lines. "Actually, it might be a little rough. But after that it'll be smooth sailing. Ready?"

"I'm putting my motor on right now," Lisa said. "My legs are still tired from yesterday."

"I'll see you cheaters at the top," Val said, taking off.

Michelle held off turning on her motor as long as she could, but a few minutes into the steep hill, she started having trouble. It was the same spot where a young couple was having an extraordinarily bad time.

The guy was still riding on his bike, albeit extremely slowly, while his wife (or girlfriend?) was walking hers, yards behind him. She'd given up, trudging along and glaring at him as he shouted half-hearted encouragements. "Come on! You can do it!"

Michelle heard the woman muttering to herself as she rode past. "Oh yeah, I can do it," the woman said. "I can get up there and kill you for making me do this."

It was too hard not to laugh. Michelle put her motor on. "Good luck, Val!" she called out as she puttered away.

"I won't need it!" Val yelled back.

The hill ended up being even longer than Michelle had expected. It was hard to tell from the map, but when she checked her watch, she saw that they'd been climbing for over a mile.

Lisa was waiting for her at the top. "I don't know how Val's going to make it."

Michelle pulled out her water. "She'll survive. We should go."

"Shell..." Lisa crossed her arms.

"What? Now we're stuck waiting for her. It's mostly downhill from here. She'll be fine."

Lisa refused to budge, and they waited for over fifteen minutes. Val eventually showed up, pushing her bike up the hill, red-faced and drenched in sweat. Her hair was stuck to her forehead.

So much for not letting a helmet mess up her hair. Michelle couldn't resist. "Piece of cake, huh?"

Val grunted. "Is this awful, stupid bike ride over yet?"

"Nope. We're just about halfway!" Michelle hopped back on her bike and took off. She didn't need the motor anymore, and they were finally getting to see Eagle Lake.

It was quiet and peaceful, the clean water framed by hills and mountains. She and Lisa stopped to take a few pictures. Val refused to participate, even though she was no longer behind. The trail was now much easier, but her mood had soured permanently, it seemed.

Michelle didn't care. It wouldn't spoil her fun.

After a short hour and a half, the bike ride was over. Michelle and Lisa returned their bikes in good spirits, while

Val dragged herself to the car, complaining she felt like she'd been hit by a truck. She sulked the entire drive back to the house.

"We have plenty of time to shower and get ready," Lisa said warily as they walked inside. "Isn't that nice?"

Val shrugged. "I guess."

"What's the big plan on getting Sam to talk to you about Lou?" asked Michelle. "Do you have anything?"

"Of course I do," Val spat back. "I'm not an idiot."

"Okay." Michelle wasn't going to ask if she was going to be so sassy about it.

They showered and changed, arriving at the restaurant promptly at eleven o'clock. It wasn't a fancy place, mostly take-out, with a few small tables.

Val led the way, walking straight up to the cash register.

"What can I get you?" asked the man behind the counter.

"I need to talk to Sam Beverly," Val said.

"Sam?" He paused, and yelled over his shoulder. "What time is Sam coming in?"

"Not until three. He's doing deliveries tonight."

The man turned back to them. "Can I get you something in the meantime?"

Val forced a smile. "No, we'll be back. Thank you."

Michelle was sick of riding the roller coaster of Val's emotions, but at least she was happy for a bit.

They went to Jordan Pond and got lunch at the restaurant there, eating outside with a view of the lake.

According to Zora's notes, Justine liked to sit here and admire the view. It was lovely, except for Val droning on and on about all the things she was going to ask Sam.

They returned to their Sam search a bit before three o'clock and grabbed a table. Lisa pulled a picture of Sam up on her phone.

Michelle studied his face. He was a young guy in his twenties. He didn't particularly look like a blackmailer, but what did she know?

When he walked through the door, Val jumped from her seat. "Sam?"

He glanced at her. "Yeah?"

"Hi. It's nice to finally meet you. I'm an admirer of your work."

A bemused smile broke his flat expression. "Thanks, I guess?"

Val leaned in, lowering her voice. "The work you've done with Lou Emerald."

The smile dropped off of his face. "I don't know what you're talking about."

Michelle cringed. Was that it? This was what Val had been planning all along?

Val followed him as he walked through the restaurant. "It's okay. I'm on your side. I'm here to help."

"I don't need your help."

"Well, yes, you do."

He stopped and looked at her. "What's your name?"

She flashed a smile. "Valerie Villano, but you can call me Val."

He nodded, pulling out his phone. "I'm calling the cops, Val. If you're not gone in five minutes, they'll arrest you for harassment."

Michelle and Lisa exchanged looks. "We'd better go."

"We're not going anywhere until we get some answers," Val growled.

The man behind the register emerged and waved his arms. "Okay, ladies. That's enough. We don't need any trouble."

Sam held his phone to his ear. "Yes, we've got some belligerent customers down at The Lobster Shack."

Val's nostrils flared and she looked like she was going to say something highly regrettable. Michelle didn't know how to stop her. She just stared with her mouth open.

Luckily, instead of insulting the kid, Val turned and stormed out, Michelle and Lisa following closely behind.

Twenty-one

They drove to the house in silence. Lisa was thankful for it. While she didn't know what to say, at least Michelle wasn't taking the opportunity to kick Val while she was down.

When they were nearly there, Lisa's phone rang, Neil's face lighting up her screen.

She ignored it, but he called back again, and again.

"Would you answer that?" Val snapped.

She winced. So much for keeping quiet. She answered his fourth call in a hushed tone. "Neil, now isn't a good time."

His voice boomed through the speaker, loud and wild and uncontrolled. "You're telling me! They just repossessed the car."

"What? Who did? Which car?"

"I don't know, the bank?" He scoffed. "Your car!"

A hot feeling ran through her. "That doesn't make any sense."

"I guess you didn't make the payments," He paused. "You've been too busy running around the country enjoying yourself instead of finding another job."

"*What?*" Lisa shut her eyes. How could her not having a job for three weeks cause the bank to take the car? She was still making the payments, she'd never fallen behind, she...

"Neil." She took a deep breath. "What did you do?"

"Nothing! I've been looking for work. I was supposed to have an interview today, but with all this commotion, I missed it."

Of course. Here they were again. He was at rock bottom – a new rock bottom. "Did you sell my car, Neil?"

Silence.

She sighed. It was wrong to leave him to his own devices. It was too much temptation. Lisa felt the shame of her selfishness washing over her. All so she could go on a fun trip? "I'm coming home. We'll figure it out."

"It's about time."

Val let out a laugh from the driver seat. "Are we supposed to believe Neil could ever hold down a job?"

Lisa shielded the phone with her hand. Neil didn't need to listen to that. It'd only make him upset. "I have to go. Bye, honey."

"But – "

She ended the call.

"I'm sorry, but we could hear everything," Val said. "The volume is too loud on your phone."

"Sorry." Lisa cleared her throat. "I need to get back home. I shouldn't have come on this trip."

Michelle turned around, her face creased with worry. "Are you having problems finding a new job? I thought that – "

"It's fine!" Lisa was surprised by how loud her own voice had grown. She took a breath and started again. "Don't worry about it. Everything is fine. I just need to go home."

"It's not fine, Lisa," Val countered. They'd just pulled up to the house. She turned off the car and turned around. "Why do you waste your life taking care of him?"

Her jaw dropped. "I'm not wasting my life. I can't just abandon the father of my children because – "

Val cut her off. "Are you going to wait until he kills you? Like Lou did to Justine?"

For goodness' sake. "Neil is not going to kill me," she said. "He's harmless. He's helpless, really."

"At least you've got that right," Val said with a snicker.

"Val!" Michelle gathered her biking gear and stood to face her. "Stop taking your bad moods out on everyone."

"Not that we could ever prove it if he did kill you," Val continued, getting out of the driver's seat. "We're three of the most useless women on earth. We're letting Justine's husband get away with murder, my husband took my career and got away with it, and your husband is like a loser teenager who can't be left alone."

"My husband isn't a loser!" Lisa had her arms at her sides, hands balled into fists. People were always attacking Neil. She was sick of it!

"He's taking everything from you."

Lisa let out a huff. "He hasn't taken anything from me!"

Val smirked before turning away. "Except your car."

"That's enough, Val!" Michelle yelled, now at Val's side.

Val shrugged and started walking toward the house. "The sooner you face it, the better off you'll be."

Lisa felt like her chest was on fire. Her breathing was off, and she couldn't think of a single thing to say.

Michelle touched her arm. "Don't listen to her. She's just a bitter has-been, blaming everyone else for her problems and drowning her sorrows in booze."

Val spun around. "What did you just say?"

Michelle stared at her. "I'm sorry your plan to confront Sam went poorly, but don't take it out on us."

"Don't act all high and mighty," Val said, wagging a finger. "Your husband was no saint either."

"No," Michelle said firmly. "He wasn't a saint. He was something better. He was real, and if he were alive today – "

"But he isn't! And you can't move past it!"

Lisa took a step back. She was too stunned to pull them off of each other. All she could do was watch.

"I can't move past it?" Michelle took a step toward her. "I've been running a successful business for the last decade. What have you done in the last decade, Val?"

"I am reviving my career!" Val yelled back.

"You don't have a career! If you had any self-awareness you would've taken that university job and – "

Val cut her off. "Oh, grow up. What do you know about universities? You couldn't even finish a year of school, and you're so terrified of leaving the island that you can't step on a plane without having a full-blown panic attack."

Michelle fell silent. Val stared at her, eyes full of fury.

Lisa's phone rang.

She glanced down. It was Neil.

She silenced it, struggling to think of something to say to stop the yelling.

"I'm not going to argue with you," Michelle said, walking to the front door the house.

Val shrugged, wandering off around the side of the house.

Lisa looked down at her phone. Another call coming in from Neil.

She shut her eyes. What a disaster this all was. It felt like she couldn't breathe again.

Lisa knew she was of no use here. It was time to go. The fun was over.

Twenty-two

Zora was a wizard. She booked Val a flight that got her out of Maine in under three hours.

Val decided to drag her bags to a nearby bar to wait it out. It ended up being the right choice. The bartender recognized her and said her drinks were on the house.

Life was good.

He slid a margarita across the counter. "What's your secret?"

The guy was a little rough around the edges. A little wild-eyed, a little sweaty. But he was a fan. An admirer. Michelle would never understand what that was like. "Secret for what?"

He smiled a wide grin. "Looking so good all these years later."

Val took a sip. It was too sweet. Not her favorite flavor, either, but at least it was free. She smiled back at him. "I know when to drop dead weight."

Twenty-three

The rest of the evening was a bust. Michelle reached out to Lisa, only to find that she was already at the airport waiting for a flight. She struggled with what to say to her and settled on wishing her a safe trip.

Val disappeared without a word. Michelle left it at that.

There was no use trying to force it. This wasn't working for any of them. Maybe the trip had been too long. Maybe the most they could take was a weekend together every few years. They were too different now. Their lives had grown too far apart, and they didn't know one another. Not truly, and it was painful to pretend otherwise.

After an internal debate, Michelle made the decision to stay behind. She wasn't done with Acadia National Park quite yet. She still hadn't gotten to drive around or hike any of the mountain trails. She still hadn't had her chance to see the sunrise on Cadillac Mountain, the one all the guidebooks raved about. And, though Zora hadn't mentioned it, the sunrise seemed like something Justine would've loved.

The event was so popular that Acadia required reservations. Michelle had made hers as soon as she knew they were coming to the island. She'd been waiting to tell Val and Lisa how early they'd have to wake up until they were in better spirits.

That time never arrived. Michelle still wanted to go, and she wouldn't be going alone. She had Justine.

It was easy to fall asleep early that night, and Michelle welcomed the physical and mental break from the day. She set her alarm for three the next morning and drifted off.

When her alarm went off, she popped out of bed, got dressed, and got on the road. It took nearly half an hour to get to the top of the mountain. Michelle drove slowly, her headlights illuminating the curves and bends in the mountain road until she finally reached the summit at 1,527 feet.

The parking lot was filling quickly, but Michelle managed to find a spot. When she got out of the car, she was immediately blasted by a powerful, biting wind.

That was something the guidebooks failed to mention. The darkness was already beginning to lift. The flashlight she'd brought was unnecessary, and Michelle carefully made her way to a spot away from the crowd.

She took a seat on a rock and a shiver ran through her. It felt like she was on the edge of the world.

The sky glowed blue, growing lighter until the first signs of the grand show appeared. It began with a deep pink cracking the horizon, touched at the edges with a light orange tone. The colors intensified before fading to an orange and yellow burn.

They were lucky it wasn't foggy; there were only a few clouds in the sky. Michelle sat, enthralled, as the sun made its first appearance from behind a cloud, highlighting the edges with a blinding sheen.

Now the world was revealed and reborn – the mountains and hills in the distance, the trees dotting the landscape in every direction, and the ocean at their feet.

It was too much to take in, and before she knew it, it was over. She sat there, the wind blowing through her ears, as the people around her got up and left.

Michelle's hips were stiff from sitting on the ground, so she too stood and stretched. She carefully picked up Justine's urn and found a quiet overlook.

"We tried, Justine," she said softly, removing the lid. "It seems like we can't make it work without you." The wind whipped the ash from her fingers before she had a chance to release it. Michelle imagined it being carried hundreds, thousands, of miles away.

For the first time since Justine's passing, Michelle couldn't hold back. Sobs bubbled from deep in her chest and tears streamed down her cheeks.

Justine was gone, as were the friendships she'd cherished so dearly.

It was over.

● ● ●

Michelle didn't know what else to do, so she spent the rest of the day hiking. She managed to ignore her thoughts by taking on increasingly challenging trails.

It worked for a while, but when she got back to the house that evening, the memory of the past two weeks was there, waiting for her.

After a shower, she decided against going into town. There was enough food in the house to make dinner, or so she thought before she spilled half a package of flavored rice onto the kitchen floor.

She let out a sigh. "Great."

There was a vacuum in the hallway closet, and to Michelle's delight, it still worked.

Yet only a few seconds after it sprung to life, it died, along with all of the other lights and appliances in the kitchen.

"Of course," she muttered. She wasn't able to reset the socket, so she had to venture down the dark, rickety basement steps to find the fusebox.

Mercifully, all of the switches were labeled clearly, and when she flipped the kitchen switch, the refrigerator hummed back to life and the microwave beeped victoriously.

Michelle slammed the fusebox shut and turned to leave. Next to the stairs, however, something caught her eye. Tucked among the boxes of Emerald junk – sweatshirts, pamphlets, and guidance books – there was a little black book with a bright blue pen sticking out from the pages.

"Oh my gosh." She grabbed the book, turning it in her hands and opening to the first page. It was another one of Justine's diaries.

She hurriedly flipped to the back to find Justine hadn't filled this one out in its entirety. There were only thirty pages or so that had been written on.

The last entry was written the day before her death.

Michelle got down on her knees, digging through the remainder of the boxes, looking for any other diaries. Once she was satisfied there were no more, she grabbed the black book and ran upstairs to the safety of the couch.

She read the last entry first, her eyes flying over the words so quickly that she had to double back to understand the meaning.

Oh diary,

I take back what I said before. My life isn't over. I feel GREAT. My guru was right. I just needed to release all of those toxins from my body before I could start healing.

Healing is what I've needed. I've been so alone. I've turned into a failure, and Lou always said people don't like being around failures. That's the real reason why no one from Emerald will return my calls. He said they're embarrassed for me.

It hurt. It did. But it was a wakeup call. My guru said I've ended up where I am because I always listen to other people over listening to myself. He said everyone – my mom, my friends,

Lou, the rest of the inconsiderate world – needs to be shut out so I can hear my own inner voice.

I'm listening now! I've been on a fruit juice only cleanse for a little over a week. It was hard at first, and the number of supplements he has me on is a little overwhelming, but now I feel AMAZING!

Michelle's heart sank. Who was this guru, and why had he forced Justine to limit her diet to juice for a week?

A knock rang out at the front door. Michelle leapt up. Maybe Lisa or Val had come back? It was perfect timing. She needed to show the diary to them. They needed to figure out who this guy was, and why Justine was listening to him, and –

Another knock on the door turned into pounding.

What was so urgent? Michelle stood, straightening her shirt before peering through the peephole.

The pounding stopped for a moment. Michelle leaned forward. She squinted into the darkness. There was no one out there.

Had she imagined it? Was she losing her mind? She needed to turn the light on so she could see, but she didn't know which switch to hit.

A dark figure appeared, moving quickly towards her. Michelle stared in horror. She could see who it was now. It wasn't Lisa, or even Val.

It was Lou.

A swift kick rattled the wooden door between them. "Open up! I know you're in there!"

Michelle covered her mouth with her hand, as though she were afraid he could hear her breathing. She couldn't stop staring through the peephole.

Surely he couldn't see her?

His nostrils flared, and he punched the door with such force that Michelle let out a scream.

She pulled away from the door. Her hands were shaking and for the first time, she saw what Val had seen.

A killer.

Twenty-four

After her first flight out of Bar Harbor was delayed by eight hours, with no end in sight, one of the airport employees offered to give Lisa a ride to a nearby hotel for the night.

She appreciated it, and she was glad Michelle wasn't with her. The very idea of mechanical issues with a plane would've destroyed any calm she'd managed to find, and even when the plane was repaired, she might not have been able to get on. Lisa decided not to tell her about it.

The hotel was more of a motel, which was fine, but a stark contrast to her recent lodgings. The next morning, she got back to the airport and was told there was another delay.

She waited.

And waited, and waited.

Her connecting flight came and went, and the next one did, too.

Apparently, this plane was really resisting being repaired. Zora apologized profusely, promising to rebook her connecting flight as soon as she got out of Maine.

Lisa reassured her, telling her not to worry. It wasn't like getting home sooner would help her get her car back. The truth was, she'd probably never get it back. She wouldn't be able to afford a new one, either. Hopefully Neil hadn't sold his car, too.

Somehow, the news of the car situation got to Sierra and midday, she called in a panic. "Mom, what happened?"

Lisa's heart sunk. "Nothing! Everything's fine! How are you?"

"Mom."

Lisa let out a sigh. That *tone*. "What?"

"I know about your car."

"Oh, that? It's fine, honey. Nothing to worry you about."

Sierra let out a sigh. "Seriously? First you mysteriously left your job, and now this? What's going on?"

"I'm having a midlife crisis."

Sierra laughed. "No you're not. I know you. This is Dad's fault, isn't it?"

"It's not his fault. He's just having a hard time."

"Mom! This is crazy! Why do you put up with this?"

Lisa shifted her weight on her hard plastic seat. This airport wasn't the best place to spend a day. She'd been eating out of the vending machine and her muscles were stiff from the bike ride. "It's not a big deal, Sierra. You shouldn't worry so much. It's just a car."

"Oh really?" She snickered. "Dad called me and said if I didn't send him money, he'd be forced to sell your car."

Lisa let out a groan. This was new – him dragging their kids into their problems. She never thought he'd stoop so low.

But that was the ever-unpleasant surprise of addiction. "I am so sorry he did that. You didn't give him any money, did you?"

"No! And now it's my fault he sold your car!"

Lisa got up to find a quieter area. The other passengers were giving her looks. "Of course it's not your fault. You know that, right? Tell me you know that."

After a moment, Sierra said, "Yeah, I know." She paused. "You know it isn't your fault either, right?"

"Of course. Your dad just needs more support. I should've been there."

"No, Mom. This was the first time you've been able to have fun in years. Why should you sacrifice that to baby him?"

She let out a sigh. Her daughter had the youthful belief that she alone knew how other people should live their lives. She'd learn one day, but that day wasn't today. "Your father and I are fine. Don't worry, okay?"

"I'm not worried about you guys."

"Good!" Lisa's own parents had divorced when she was eleven, and she'd promised herself she would never make her kids worry about things like that.

She was doing the best she could, but Sierra seemed to worry no matter what. It was in her nature.

Sierra spoke again. "I'm worried about *you*."

"Me?" Lisa laughed. "I'm fine! I just had a wonderful trip and – "

"If you don't want me to have to put up with Dad, why are you putting up with him?"

Lisa could feel a headache coming on. This is what she got for sending her daughter off to school. She came back full of ideas. "You're the kid, I'm the adult. Remember?"

"Why, though?" Sierra's voice was pleading. "Why do you put up with it, Mom? After everything he's done? Everything he will do?"

"Well, I love him and – he's your father, and, you know, just because he has a problem I wouldn't – it's not like what you see in the movies."

Sierra was quiet for a moment. Lisa was terrified of what she would say next.

"I just want you to be happy, Mom."

Lisa forced a smile. "I am happy!"

Quiet for a moment, then, "I hope so. I have to go. I'll talk to you later?"

"Sure. Of course."

"Bye."

Lisa went back to her seat and saw her flight had been canceled.

Oy. What a day.

She went to the counter and discovered the lone employee being berated by a middle-aged woman. Lisa stood behind her until she ran out of steam and stormed off.

"I guess she's done taking her tantrum out on you," Lisa said as she stepped up.

The woman offered a weary smile. "I hope so."

She rebooked her flight for the next day, then debated what to do next. It seemed silly to go back to the motel for another night. Michelle might still be at the house. She wouldn't have wanted to fly out any sooner than she had to.

Wouldn't it be better to spend some time with her? Better than sitting in that motel room alone with her thoughts, wondering if Neil had been taking advantage of her all these years?

Divorce was impossible. As much as she wished it was an option at times, the kids needed their dad. And Neil clearly needed her. She was the one who held it all together.

Yes, some time with Michelle would be nice. She called Michelle's phone, but it didn't even ring. She might be at the house with no service.

It was worth checking in at the house. It was getting dark, and Michelle would be back from any adventures she'd taken.

Lisa ordered an Uber and when they got to the driveway, the driver asked if she'd be willing to get out and walk. "It's hard for me to turn around in these long driveways some-times."

"Oh, of course! No problem. Have a nice night."

She got her suitcase out of the back, and once the car pulled away, she realized how dark it was under the trees. She slowly walked toward the house, telling herself not to be creeped out as her bag bumped along behind her.

The rocks couldn't be good for her suitcase's wheels, but she realized it didn't matter. She wouldn't be traveling again anytime soon.

She finally caught sight of the windows glowing in the darkness. Michelle was still there! The car was there, too.

Even if Val were there, it would be okay. They could talk things out. Lisa didn't want hard feelings between them. Now that they'd all calmed down, they could...

Wait a minute.

There was another car pulled up to the side of the house. The driver's door was open and the engine was still running. It was a Mercedes.

And there was someone...yelling? It sounded like?

Lisa moved to the grass so whoever it was couldn't hear her coming. She crept closer and the shouting grew louder.

"Open this door *now!* You have no right to be in this house. No right!"

She gasped. It was Lou, pounding his fists on the doors.

Was Michelle inside?

Lisa, hands shaking, pulled her phone out of her purse and promptly dropped it on the gravel.

Lou didn't notice, thankfully, as he was making enough noise of his own.

She dropped down to her knees and dialed 911.

She pressed the phone to her ear, listening to silence for what felt like thirty seconds.

She pulled the phone away to look at it. It was struggling to connect, proclaiming it had no service.

Of course.

Lou fell silent, and Lisa squinted in the darkness to watch him. He'd moved to another door – the basement door – and started pounding on it with both fists. After a moment, he took a step back and kicked at the doorknob.

She'd never seen someone act so violently in real life. He was in a rage! She needed to do something, anything.

Lisa turned to run to the nearest neighbor's house. She took a few steps before realizing it might take too long and Lou might get into the house.

She told herself to stop and think.

Her heart was pounding in her ears. What was she supposed to do? Could she distract him? Could she attack him?

No, that wouldn't work.

Lisa looked up. The Mercedes was just sitting there. She could pop right in and...

It was now or never. Lisa ran, abandoning her bag and purse, breath high and tight in her chest.

Lou didn't see her until she'd already gotten into the front seat, pulled the door shut, and locked the car. Rage flashed across his face and he ran toward her, screaming.

Lisa screamed back as she threw the car into reverse. She slammed into the rental car, then shakily put the car into drive, shooting forward surprisingly quickly.

Lou had reached her and bashed his fists on the hood, demanding she get out. It made her jump, and the car jolted forward, nearly running him over. She hit the brakes and hurriedly reversed again.

This time, she got past the rental car. Lou gave chase, but quickly lost her as she wildly spun onto the road, then sped off in search of help.

Twenty-five

B ack on her own dime, Val elected to take the bus home
from the airport. It was a long ride, particularly with
her two large bags and the dirty looks people kept shooting at
her.

She didn't care. She was sick of people's opinions.

When she got home, she was immediately hit with an
unpleasant stench. Mothball-esque, almost like her grandma's
house used to smell.

Did her apartment always smell like this? Did *she* smell
like this?

No. It couldn't be.

Val flopped onto the couch and pulled a pile of mail onto
her lap. She'd feel better once this junk was taken care of.
That was probably where the stench was coming from,
anyway.

She tossed the coupon fliers, pizza menus, and offers for
life insurance into one pile, and the handful of actual letters
into another.

Most of these were still junk, but in disguise. She tore the
envelopes and letters to pieces, setting aside a bill for a recent
ultrasound. She'd found a lump and was thankful it was

benign, but now she had to find a way to pay for that peace of mind.

The last envelope in the pile was large and thick. It had her ex-husband's handwriting on it. Her heart leapt. She tore it open, scanning his words as quickly as she could.

Dear Valerie,

I hope you're well. I'm signing over the remaining rights to your music catalog. I know you'll put these songs to the best use, and I hope it serves you well. Wishing you all the best, always.

Yours,

Reggie

Val scoffed. Who did he think he was, taking the high road like that?

She flipped to the next page, then the next. There were photocopied pages of proof.

Pft. Val wasn't buying it. He could have faked all of it! She'd have to show her attorney to be sure.

That wouldn't be cheap. Maybe that was Reggie's game, forcing her to create more billable hours for her attorney? Seemed like something he would do.

That was enough mail for today.

She took the junk and threw it into the trash, then turned to unpacking her bags. There was still enough time in the day that she could get a load of clothes washed and dried, as long as all of the machines weren't taken. That would help her feel better.

Down she went, carrying her basket past the broken elevator, down the stairs, and into the dimly lit laundry room. There was exactly one washer open.

Perfect! Val popped her clothes in, then went back upstairs.

The smell in her apartment persisted.

She lit a candle, then, unsatisfied, threw the windows open. Someone was playing a bagpipe outside, though, so that was no good either.

Val went into her bedroom and shut the door. Maybe some music would make her feel better. Maybe an 80's playlist?

No. That didn't work. Every song was annoying.

She put on classical music. That didn't soothe her either.

What was her problem? Why wasn't she more relaxed after her long, luxurious trip?

Was it because her friends weren't speaking to her? Was it because her soon-to-be-ex-husband wasn't fighting her for the music rights? There was no way he was giving them to her just to be nice.

He probably thought the songs were worthless. Just like her friends thought her songs were worthless. They thought *she* was worthless.

Who was she kidding? She was worthless. She was a washed-up nobody with no prospects, living in a stinking third-floor apartment that smelled like old. She wasn't even allowed to have a cat, and she desperately wanted a cat.

She was completely and utterly alone, lashing out and attacking anyone who hinted at the truth of her reality.

It couldn't get any worse than this.

April 8th, 2022

*D*ear diary,
Today is my fiftieth birthday and I have no one to spend it with. I know there's no one to blame but myself.

I'm getting more used to the idea of being divorced, but not to being alone. Lou and I spent so much time apart that it was almost a natural progression for our relationship to end.

I don't blame him. We grew into our own lives, lives that didn't have room for each other. Why can't a twenty-seven-year marriage be seen as a success? Just because it didn't last forever?

I know I am the master of my fate. I hear this mantra. I repeat it. I need to own it.

It's time for me to admit I am unhappy. I have no one to blame but myself, and I'm not looking to throw a pity party, diary, but I don't know how I ended up here.

Somehow, I haven't been able to pull myself out of this slump. My days all blend together. I wake up alone, I eat alone, and I go to bed alone.

Some of my friends from Emerald still reach out. They want to talk, want to visit. How can I, though? I don't want them to see me like this. I'm not part of that community *anymore. That's Lou's thing. It was always Lou's thing, if I'm being honest.*

I've gone so long without being honest with myself. I don't have a "thing." I have nothing and no one. I know that sounds dramatic, but it's true! What have I spent my life working toward? To this? I am so ashamed. I can't talk about it. I can't even leave the house...

All this time I told myself I was living the life of my dreams. Now I know that's not true. The reality is that I hid behind the safety of Emerald. It was never my dream to build the Emerald Way to what it is today, not really.

When was the last time I helped someone, truly helped them? If only I had dared to think of things for my own life. If only I'd dared to dream.

I've decided my shameful moping needs to end. Today, on my fiftieth birthday, I am giving myself the gift of honesty. I am unhappy, this is true.

But I can fix it! I can! I found a group called the Rock Bottom Dreamers. They help people who have hit their rock bottom to find their dreams again. Simple enough, right?

It makes sense to me. Today I took the first step and made an appointment with a guru. I am not giving up. I am starting over. Wish me luck!

- Justine

Twenty-six

Outside was quiet. Too quiet. Michelle sat upstairs in total darkness. She'd turned off the lights so Lou couldn't see her.

After a moment, she looked cautiously out the window. Lou was gone. He'd stopped attacking the doors and disappeared.

Or maybe he'd found a way in?

Shoot. Why had she gone to the second floor? There was no escape from there.

The sound of a car rolling down the driveway drifted in. Michelle stared out the window, the sound of her breathing filling her ears.

It was the Mercedes.

Her chest tightened. If only her phone would work. She wanted to call someone, anyone, for help.

Instead, all she could do was watch. A truck pulled up behind the Mercedes and a man got out. The other driver joined him and they walked toward the house.

Michelle squinted in the darkness. She didn't recognize the man. The other person was a woman.

Not any woman. Lisa!

Michelle ran down the stairs and pulled the front door open, calling out to her. "I'm in here!"

Lisa ran, throwing her arms around Michelle's neck. "Are you okay?"

"I think so. Where's Lou?"

Lisa shook her head. "I've no idea. He must've run off."

"Thank goodness. Lisa, I think he was going to kill me!"

The man who had followed Lisa tilted his hat. "Ma'am. I heard you were having some trouble?"

She stared at him. He had a chiseled jaw and a broad set of shoulders – far too good looking for Michelle to process right now. Michelle was startled by her own reaction to him. "Uh, yes. Thanks for coming. The previous owner was trying to break the door down."

He nodded, his handsome face lined by a frown. "He was my neighbor. Never liked the guy. Luke, was it?"

"Lou," Lisa corrected. "He's not going to be happy once he sees what I did to his car."

The man smiled and winked. "Best not to mention that when the police arrive."

Lisa nodded, eyes wide. "Oh. Of course."

A patrol car with two officers pulled up a few minutes later. The handsome neighbor went off to greet them, all smiles and laughs. They knew each other.

Of course. It was like San Juan. Everyone knew each other.

The officers were polite, and when they came to speak to her, Michelle described what had happened. Lisa also gave her side of the story, wisely leaving out the part where she'd stolen Lou's car and almost run him over.

Michelle wasn't absolutely sure they hadn't been wrong to stay in the house, though. Was it possible Lou had gotten this house in the divorce? Were they trespassing?

She decided to give Zora a quick call to check, and Zora answered right away, full of apologies. "I had no idea Lou was in the area. I'm so sorry. It's such a mess."

"It's okay. The police officer needs to know if Lou has any rights to be on the property."

"Absolutely not."

Michelle let out a sigh. That was a relief. "Who owns it now, Zora?"

"Ah," Zora paused. "I do. Justine left it to me. I can talk to the police, if you need?"

Well. That was something. "Yeah. I think I'll put you on with him in a second. I just also – thank you. It was really nice of you to let us stay here."

"It was my pleasure. It's the least I could do."

Michelle wasn't sure about that. The least she could've done was nothing – not organize the memorial, or their trip, or any of this.

Unless Zora had done it all out of guilt.

No. Michelle wasn't going to go down that path. Silly theories were Val's thing, not hers.

"Is the officer still there?" Zora asked.

"Oh, yes." She walked over and interrupted Lisa, who sounded like she was getting dangerously close to ratting herself out. "Here is the owner of the house."

Michelle handed off the phone and pulled Lisa aside.

"I just found out Zora owns the house."

"Really?" Lisa nodded, impressed. "Good for her."

"Yeah..."

Lisa leaned in and dropped her voice. "I didn't tell the police about the car. I thought Lou was going to kill you. I panicked! I didn't mean to steal his car and run it into the – "

She waved a hand. "You did great. Don't worry about it. I don't think you're getting in trouble for it. Zora got us insurance on the rental, so it doesn't matter. It's all fine."

Lisa let out a sigh. She stared at Michelle, a small smile passing her face. "What do you think of Mister Hunky Neighbor? He seemed to like you."

Michelle rolled her eyes. "Okay, thank you. That's enough."

"What if we invited him to – "

"No." Michelle looked at her and laughed. This was all too absurd.

"I'm just kidding, sorry. Bad joke. He was just so willing to help and he got in that big truck and..."

"I *know!*" Michelle stifled a smile. "I'm not blind."

They laughed quietly, the pressure of the moment lifting.

Michelle cleared her throat. "There's something I need to show you."

Lisa cocked her head to the side. "Okay?"

Just then, they heard commotion outside. It seemed Lou had returned to the property, ranting and raving, and had been promptly arrested.

Hunky Neighbor Guy laughed as Lou's face was pressed into the dirt during handcuffing.

"When everyone is gone, I'll show you." Michelle added.

Lisa nodded. "Got it."

● ● ●

Once the excitement was over and Michelle and Lisa were left to themselves, they locked the doors and convened in the kitchen.

Lisa turned to her. "Are you afraid? We can go somewhere else. I found a run-down motel you wouldn't enjoy."

Michelle laughed, walking back to the front door. "I'm not afraid anymore." She picked up the diary from the floor. She dropped it in her panic. "I need you to see this."

"What is it?" Lisa had taken a seat at the kitchen island and poured herself a glass of red wine. She offered some to Michelle.

"No thanks. Look." Michelle lifted the notebook in her hands. "This is Justine's last diary."

"What!" Lisa reached out a hand. "Can I see?"

"Yeah. I only got a chance to read the last entry before Lou showed up."

Lisa nodded, flipping too far initially before finding her place. She read the entry, then looked up at Michelle. "Who's this guru she keeps talking about?"

"I don't know."

Lisa frowned. "Do you think Zora knew about him?"

Michelle hadn't thought of that. "Maybe. I don't know if Zora is..."

"What?"

"I don't even want to say this out loud," Michelle said. She dropped her voice to a whisper. "What if Zora isn't trustworthy?"

Lisa's mouth popped open. "*Michelle!* You're starting to sound like Val!"

"I know," she said with a groan. "I think this whole night got to me. I feel unstable."

Lisa took a swig of wine. "I doubt Zora was anything but unflinchingly loyal to Justine, but let's call her and ask. See how she reacts."

"That's a terrible idea!" Michelle stared at her. "What if we upset her?"

"I don't mean accuse her of anything. Just, you know, ask about the guru, and what happened to Justine."

This was silly. They needed to wait until their nerves calmed down. Otherwise, they might do something they would regret.

As Michelle silently debated what to do, Lisa put her phone on speaker and made the call.

Michelle reached over, frantically trying to hang up, but it was too late. Zora had answered. "Hey! Are you ladies okay?"

"We're fine. Thanks, Zora," Lisa said. "I just wanted to update you that the police arrested Lou for trespassing."

"I know. I saw."

Michelle tilted her head to the side. "You did?"

Zora let out a laugh. "Lou had cameras installed all around the property, and I've kept them running. I figured it was good to keep an eye on things."

"Oh," Lisa said, nodding. "That's good. Well, we found a — hang on."

"What?" asked Zora.

Michelle mouthed, "No!" at Lisa, who continued ignoring her.

"Were there cameras here when Justine died?"

Michelle smacked Lisa in the arm, but it was too late.

"Yes," Zora said. "Justine was – " Her voice cracked, and she cleared her throat. "There aren't cameras inside the house, but the ones we have give a pretty good idea of what Justine's last day was like."

"You don't have to talk about this," Michelle said.

"No, it's okay. You should know. Justine was alone all day. She left once in the morning. The cameras showed her coming back with a few grocery bags."

"Had you talked to her at all?" asked Lisa.

"No. She was doing a digital detox. She'd stopped answering her phone and I hadn't heard from her in two weeks."

"A digital detox," Michelle repeated.

"It was all because of that guru," Zora said, voice dripping with disdain. "I was so worried when I hadn't heard from her that I showed up here, unannounced, and tried to find out what was going on. She seemed okay, except for being manic and overexcited. I tried to talk her out of being so extreme with what she was doing, but she wouldn't hear it. She was on a juice-only diet and taking a dozen guru-approved supplements a day. Though she looked a bit gaunt, she seemed happy. Giddy, even."

Michelle frowned. That all sounded about right for one of Justine's "health" kicks – she always took things to the extreme.

"Did the guru do something to her?" Lisa asked.

"I don't think so," Zora said. "He was never here, and that was the last time I saw her. The next week, Lou showed up at the house. He was the one who found her."

Lisa gasped. "*Found* her?"

"Yes." Zora paused. "He still had a key and...well, he let himself in and came out screaming a moment later."

Michelle leaned forward. "Did Lou hurt her?"

"No. She was already gone."

They were silent for a moment. Michelle looked at Lisa. Her face was twisted, and her lip was quivering. She was no longer in charge of this conversation.

"What happened to Justine?" Michelle asked as gently as she could.

"We're not sure," Zora said. "Lou had sent Justine an email asking if he could borrow the house for an investor's visit. Justine would have said yes, normally, but she wasn't checking her email or responding to him. He assumed she was busy and just showed up."

"Sounds like Lou," Michelle muttered under her breath.

"He was in a hurry and ordered dinner to be delivered for him and his guest when he got here, a lobster delivery. After Lou ran out of the house in a panic, the delivery boy showed up a minute later."

"Wait, Zora," Lisa interrupted. "Was the delivery guy someone named Sam Beverly?"

"I'm not sure. I have the videos if you want to see him. Why?"

"No reason," Lisa said. "We, uh, met a Sam Beverly here."

"It could be," Zora said. "I never spoke to him. Lou sent him away before making an anonymous 911 call."

"Why anonymous?" asked Michelle. "What was he trying to hide?"

"I think he was worried it would look suspicious," Zora said. "He has no idea I have access to the cameras. Though I'm guessing he figured it out when he realized you were visiting."

Lisa let out a long "Ooh."

"That makes a lot of sense," Michelle said. "But how can we be sure Lou didn't hurt Justine?"

"He was in the house for less than thirty seconds," Zora said. "The police found no signs of a struggle."

"What happened, then?" Michelle asked.

"We don't know. We're still waiting on the autopsy." Zora took a deep breath. "The police said it looked like she was in the middle of making a smoothie in the blender and just collapsed."

Michelle sat back. "Poor Justine."

"Poor Justine," Lisa repeated, nodding solemnly.

"I'm so sorry Lou came after you like that," Zora continued. "I think he's afraid the videos will get out and make him look guilty. I should have told you about it, but I didn't want to spoil your trip and – "

"It's not your fault," Michelle said. "That's just Lou."

"I'm still sorry," she continued. "I miss her every day. I wish I'd done everything differently."

"You were a wonderful friend to her," Lisa said. "Don't be sorry. She loved you."

"She loved you very much, too. I'm sorry the trip ended this way."

Michelle shook her head. "Don't be. We had the most wonderful time, Zora. Thank you." She paused. "We won't bother you anymore tonight. Thanks for all of your help."

"We can talk tomorrow?"

"Sure. Goodnight."

Michelle ended the call and looked at Lisa. "Well. There it is."

Lisa nodded. "There it is."

"Val is going to be devastated."

Lisa cracked a smile. "You're right. But maybe now she can move on."

Michelle grabbed a wine glass. "No. It won't help." She poured a heavy glass and took a sip. "It actually doesn't make me feel better at all."

Twenty-seven

Their flight out of Bar Harbor went off without a hitch. Lisa was thankful her earlier flights had been canceled —it had all worked out in the end.

With Lisa's help, Michelle wrote an email to Val explaining what they'd found out about Lou. She also included an invitation to San Juan Island to spread the last of Justine's ashes in a few weeks.

"She won't come," Michelle said after she sent the email. "She's too proud."

Lisa shrugged it off. "That's not the point."

"Aren't you still mad at her?" asked Michelle.

After reading those last, lonely entries in Justine's diary, Lisa didn't have an ounce of anger left. Justine had needed her, and she'd failed to be there for her.

Val needed her, too, even if she would never admit it.

Lisa smiled. "No. I'm not mad. I know she didn't mean what she said. I'll give her some time to cool down, but she won't get rid of me that easily."

Michelle let out a sigh. "Oh, you. Never change, Lisa."

"I wasn't planning on it!"

Without the excitement of a new destination ahead of them, the flight felt much calmer. Even Michelle seemed more subdued, not needing her headphones or eye mask to relax. She was quiet and seemed lost in her thoughts.

They connected through Boston, then made the flight back to Seattle. Lisa offered to split a cab with Michelle, but she declined.

"Arthur is picking me up," she said with a sheepish smile.

Lisa knew better than to push Michelle too much on that topic. It was a big deal for Michelle to even entertain the idea of a male suitor.

Lisa settled with saying, "I'd like a chance to get to know him better."

Michelle responded airily, "I think I'd like you to have the chance to get to know him better, too."

They hugged and parted ways. Lisa felt a bit weepy, but reminded herself it was just for now, not forever.

To no one's surprise, Neil had not offered to pick Lisa up at the airport. He was using one of his favorite techniques to get her attention: the silent treatment.

As tempting as it was to ignore him right back, it was time to go home.

When she got to the house, she was hit with quite a sight – and smell. The kitchen was in shambles. There were multiple caked-on layers of food on the stovetop – pasta sauce, cheese, and were those lentils?

The sink and dishwasher were full of dishes, all dirty, and the trash was overflowing. The living room had a pizza box splayed open on the floor, and the dining room table was covered in boxes, unopened mail, and dirty laundry.

It was like their home had been overtaken by a bunch of frat boys. She let out a sigh. Neil spiraled like this sometimes, and there was no use in arguing with him. He'd tell her she was unpleasant to be around, then blame her for whatever he'd done.

These spells didn't last forever – it wasn't the real him that acted like this. It was just when he got trapped in these low points of despair. She reminded herself it, too, would pass and her cheerful husband would return.

Neil was nowhere to be seen now. He knew she was coming home and was clearly avoiding her.

That was fine. It gave her time to tidy up. Lisa went upstairs to fetch a laundry basket and discovered the worst betrayal of all. Both Avery and Sierra's rooms were almost entirely empty. Their TVs, desks, and even their bed frames and mattresses were gone.

How would she explain this to them? How could they come home and visit if their beds had been sold off?

Sierra had loved that bed. She'd bought it with her own money, years ago, after seeing it in a magazine. She always loved decorating and making things her own.

For him to sell it off like that... well, it was enough to make Lisa drop to the floor and weep.

She didn't cry for long, though. There was too much work to be done.

It took nearly three hours to tidy up the kitchen and living room, then another hour for the dining room. She managed to get four loads of laundry washed and folded, then turned her attention to her suitcase.

That was tough. Every time she pulled something out of it, she remembered where she'd worn it and where they'd been. She'd accidentally taken Val's shirt from their cleaning escapade. She'd have to return it, but some small part of her wanted to keep it.

Lisa sat on the floor, her suitcase empty, and started flipping through pictures on her phone. At the time, it seemed like they were taking a million pictures too many. Now, alone and back in the routine of her life, she wished she'd taken more.

She made up her mind to gather Val and Michelle's pictures and compile them into a photo book. She'd make one for each of them to commemorate the trip. It would be a good way to patch things up, too.

Neil came home when she was still gazing through her pictures, misty-eyed. When she heard the front door open, she stood to meet him.

"Hi, Neil," she said wearily from the top of the stairs.

He didn't even look at her as he walked past, stomping up the stairs before shutting himself in their bedroom.

Terrific. He was in a mood. Of course he was. He'd made a big mess and left it for her to clean, and now he was the upset one.

Lisa didn't want to deal with him. She carried the laundry down and got back to folding.

After that, she made herself a quick dinner and worked up the courage to make a video call to the kids. She braced herself as she told them the bad news, finishing with, "But don't worry. We can get all new stuff and it'll be a lot more comfortable when you visit."

Sierra spoke first, rolling her eyes. "Don't worry about that, Mom. I don't care about the bed."

"You loved that bed!" Lisa said.

"Yeah, when I was like fifteen. We can get another bed."

Whew. A weight lifted from her shoulders.

Avery seemed to agree. "Yeah, Mom. My TV only worked half the time anyway."

She smiled. Her kids had never been into material things. Lisa didn't know how she managed to raise them that way, but she was grateful. "I'm sorry about all this. We'll figure it out."

"It sucks, Mom," Avery said. He let out a sigh. "It's... yeah. It's bad."

Lisa nodded. "Just a few bumps in the road. Nothing more."

"Are you and Dad getting a divorce?" Avery asked.

Sierra's mouth popped open, as did Lisa's.

"What?" Avery shrugged. "We're all thinking it."

"I would never do that to you kids," Lisa said firmly. "We're going to get this under control. We'll replace everything – "

"I don't care about the stuff," Sierra said. "Avery doesn't either. Like I said, Mom, I worry about you."

Lisa shook her head. Not this again. "Sierra, like I told you – "

Avery cut her off. "Just divorce him already, Mom."

Lisa was stunned into silence. She dropped her voice to a whisper. "What?"

He made a face. "I mean, I feel sorry for Dad, but I don't know. I'm twenty-five, I'm an actual adult – "

"An actual adult, eh?" Lisa had to stifle a laugh. "That sounds like something an adult would say."

He broke into a smile. "You know what I mean. It's just like, you know, Dad acts like it's so hard and...I don't know. It isn't that hard not to be a total jerk."

Lisa let out a sigh. His gambling addiction made things harder. It always had. It wasn't *him*, though. It was the illness. It was the addiction. Still, Lisa had to admit that at times it was hard to tell who he was anymore.

She cleared her throat. "Life is hard, Avery."

"It doesn't have to be," Sierra said. "I mean, obviously this is your life, and I know that I'm the kid and you're the adult, and whatever. But if you're only staying with Dad because of us, I want you to know you don't have to. Okay?"

Lisa's vision got cloudy again. Today was a weepy day, that was for sure. "I don't want you to worry. Just promise me that, okay?"

Sierra sighed. "Okay."

"I've got to run," Avery said. "I'll call you later?"

"Sure."

"Just think about it, Mom," Sierra added. "Think about yourself for once."

She forced a smile and nodded. "Yes, yes. I have a lot to think about. Be good."

For the first time during the entire conversation, Sierra smiled. "Good. I love you! Bye!"

"Love you!" Avery added before disappearing from the call.

Her phone went dark just as the laundry went off.

She was about to get it, but then stopped herself. Instead, she grabbed her laptop and settled onto the couch. If she only dared to dream...

Twenty-eight

Val's email became quite the source of angst over the next few days. First was Michelle's long message about Lou returning to the house, Lisa coming to her rescue, and the arrest of the famous Mr. Emerald.

All of that was extremely enjoyable to read, especially since she'd expected Michelle's email to be a long, well-deserved scolding.

There was no scolding at all, actually, and the less fun part of the email came second. Michelle claimed to have a new theory about Justine's death.

On first pass, Val found it all hard to believe. Justine had been sad, sure, and she'd found some kooky new guru to follow, but how did that lead to her death? How did they know Lou hadn't messed with the cameras to look innocent?

Val wasn't convinced. She and Tammy were waiting on the coroner's report.

Finally, at the very end, Michelle invited her to come back to San Juan Island to spread Justine's ashes at her favorite park.

That was kind, sort of, but how was Val supposed to face them after the things she said?

Anyway, she didn't have enough money for a plane ticket. She was pathetic.

She didn't know what to say, so she simply didn't respond.

A week later she was busy cleaning houses and trying to bury Debbie's bad review on Skillz when she got another interesting email.

This one was from Chloe. The girl didn't know when to quit, and Val loved that about her.

Apparently, Chloe had been so disgusted by Lou that she launched a campaign to find more of his wrongdoings in the Emerald community.

"I had to be careful, because as you know, the entire Emerald community is a mix of dedication and paranoia. But I found people willing to talk."

Val called her and they spoke for nearly two hours. Chloe was a smart cookie. She knew who to trust, and she knew who to tiptoe around.

One of the accountants who volunteered her time for Emerald – because Lou didn't pay anyone he didn't have to – had noticed some suspicious activity, but she didn't know whom to tell. She was relieved when Chloe came asking questions and provided some documents to her.

"She's scared of Lou, though. They all are," Chloe said. "Except me. He's got nothing on me."

Chloe pieced together that Lou had been funneling money from donations and sessions into fake expenses. He'd even created phony companies to pay for various services – consulting, advertising, security. None of them were real. Lou owned all of the companies, and he barely made an effort to hide the fact. All of the money was going to him.

"I think he's flat broke. He spends every penny he gets, on new cars, or trips, or mansions. He was nagging everyone about not recruiting enough, not volunteering enough hours and not having enough conferences and retreats. Meanwhile, he's draining the Emerald community for all they have."

This was music to Val's ears. "You have to tell them."

It was there that Chloe's courage faltered. "I know, but people will think I'm just a bitter ex-girlfriend. I don't know what I want to happen. A lot of my friends are still faithful Emeralds. I think we could rebuild a great organization if we could only get rid of Lou. I just don't know how yet."

"Well, you think about it, and I'll think about a way to bring him down."

Chloe laughed. "Deal."

Val was so excited that she nearly called Michelle and Lisa to tell them the good news, but then she remembered she'd ruined their friendship.

They wouldn't want to hear it. They wouldn't want to get dragged into another scheme, even if they still wanted to be her friend. Michelle's email had been polite but reserved.

Val couldn't respond in kind. She was going to let it all out. After a week, she finally found a way to answer.

Dear Michelle and Lisa,

    I'm sorry for everything I said. There's no excuse, but I take it back. Remember that? When we used to take things back? I know it doesn't work for things like this, but I wish it did.

    I would like to come for Justine's final goodbye, but to tell you the truth, I'm broke.

    There you have it. You were right. I am a mess. I don't know why I tried to lie to you, or to myself, but... yeah.

    It's not much, but I'm hoping I can make it up to both of you when I get back at Lou. Even if he didn't kill Justine, he deserves to pay.

Yours always,

Val

After she hit send, she realized it was probably a bad idea to put threats into writing like that.

Oh well!

It was too late, and she wasn't *actually* going to kill him. That wasn't her style.

She was a mess, that was true, but at least she had a purpose again.

Twenty-nine

It was another beautiful day in Friday Harbor. They had a high temperature of seventy-four degrees, white puffy clouds in the sky, and crisp, clean air.

Michelle stood on the sidewalk across from the ferry landing, leaning against the wall and basking in the morning sun. She hoped it would be a good day.

The green and white ferry had made its appearance in the distance a few minutes ago and was now moving almost imperceptibly slowly toward her.

Michelle smiled. She was grateful she wasn't the one traveling today. The fun was coming to her.

The excitement around her rose once the ferry docked. She wasn't the only one waiting for passengers, and a nearby five-year-old repeated, "Daddy's coming home today! Daddy's coming home today!" in a sing-song voice.

People began streaming off the ferry, bags in tow and smiles on their faces. They jumped into waiting cars, onto mopeds and trolleys, and into the arms of the people waiting nearby.

Finally, Michelle spotted her two charges: Lisa and Val, the last ones in line.

She stuck a hand in the air and waved. "Over here!"

Lisa's face brightened into a smile and she almost stepped in front of a car trying to cross the street. Val's face was mostly obstructed by her enormous hat, but she, too, was smiling.

"I didn't know you'd be waiting for us," Lisa said when she'd reached the sidewalk safely. "I thought we'd just stop by the café and surprise you."

"Oh, come on!" Michelle pulled her in for a hug. "I had to prepare a welcome for my guests."

Val nodded. "I was hoping to get a welcome from Tammy, actually. Where is she?"

Michelle laughed, giving her a hug too. "I invited her, but she said just to bring the leftover ashes for her mantel."

"Aw." Lisa's face twisted into a frown. "It's too much for her."

"I know. But I will not be the one delivering them." Michelle offered to take Val's bag, but she declined. "The last time I stepped by to check on her, she yelled at me through the window for almost ten minutes. Said I stepped on her flowers."

Val whipped her hat off and slipped on a pair of oversized sunglasses. "Don't worry, I'll do it. I'm not afraid of Tammy anymore. We understand each other now."

Michelle nodded. There was no need to discuss what she meant. Tammy had finally received the coroner's report and shared it exclusively with Val.

Justine's cause of death was an intracranial hemorrhage –
a brain bleed. She'd had high levels of various chemicals in her
blood, suspected to be from the supplements the guru had
instructed her to take. The supplements were unsafe on their
own, but doubly unsafe for someone on a blood thinner with
a history of a stroke. The theory was that the supplements
interacted with Justine's blood thinner and caused the cata-
strophic bleed.

Val had shared the results with them in an email, finally
admitting that Lou wasn't a murderer. Tammy had laid the
theory to rest, too, but she and Val still kept in touch as
though they were old pen pals.

After gathering their bags, Michelle led her friends down
the street to the cafe's upstairs apartment. She was excited to
unveil the fancy brunch she'd put together for them. "Ta-da!"

"Well, isn't this beautiful!" Lisa said as she walked in the
room.

"Thank you." Michelle took their bags and set them out
of the way. "I have some old favorites and some new recipes
I've been testing out. I got the ideas from our travels."

Val took a seat. "I thought I was the one who's supposed
to get ideas from our travels."

Lisa and Michelle chuckled and took their seats. Then
something terrible happened.

They all fell silent.

Michelle's heart rate picked up. Was it going to be awkward now? A bad day? After all they'd been through, was the magic gone?

Val cleared her throat. "Well, I'll start. I want to apologize to both of you for how I behaved, and for the things I said."

Lisa leaned forward, grabbing her by the arm. "Consider yourself forgiven."

Michelle nodded. "Water under the bridge."

"No, it really wasn't okay. I was nasty, and you didn't deserve it." She let out a sigh. "It was my fault, and I take full responsibility. I've been spiraling for a while, but I couldn't admit it to myself. I wanted to blame everyone else – the industry, Reggie, Lou, and when I ran out of targets, I turned on you two."

Michelle shrugged. "At least you were efficient."

They all laughed and the tension seemed to crack.

Val went on. "The truth is, I've been broken, and broke, for a long time. I've been cleaning houses and teaching singing lessons, barely getting by, clinging to a dream of the person I once was."

"Broke?" Lisa gaped at her. "You flew into the memorial on a helicopter!"

Val paused, then let out a laugh. "Oh, that? The pilot is a friend of mine – he's a stuntman, flies helicopters on the side. He owed me a favor."

"You had me fooled," Lisa said.

Val turned to her. "I'm so sorry about what I said about Neil. I think I've been bitter about my own divorce, just refusing to accept that fact that we fell out of love and – "

"No, hang on." Lisa set her tea cup down with a clatter. "You were right, Val. Neil and I aren't good for each other."

Michelle's mouth popped open and she covered it with her hand. She didn't dare say a word.

"No, no," Val sputtered, "It was about me, not you."

Lisa picked up a scone, breaking off a corner and shoving it into her mouth. "Yeah, but it was about me, too. I'm not good for Neil. My help has never helped him. I've been hiding things for years, trying to cover up for him so he wouldn't feel bad, so people wouldn't see what he was like when he was at his worst. And you know what? He never made a real effort to get help. How could he, when all I did was run after him, cleaning up messes?"

Michelle stared at her, wide-eyed. "What have you been hiding?"

"Oh, everything!" Lisa took another bite and laughed. "I'm almost broke, too. Neil figured out how to steal money from my old company and got me fired. I almost ended up in prison, but I managed to pay them back."

"Lisa!" Michelle dropped her voice. "If you need money, I can help you."

"She's good for it," Val said with a nod. "She paid my way so I could come here. By the way, Michelle, I'm paying you back."

"Absolutely not," Michelle said. "It was a gift."

"Aw!" Lisa smiled at her. "That was sweet of you, Shell."

"You know me, so sweet." She laughed. Michelle didn't want the money back. She was just glad Val had come. "Sorry, Lisa. You were saying?"

She smiled. "I don't need money, but thank you. I've got a new job. It's been great, and before, I'd been saving part of my paycheck in a secure account Neil can't access."

Val made a face. "Wow. I'm impressed."

Lisa waved a hand. "Oh, don't be. I still watched as he gambled almost everything else away. He sold my car and most of the kids' stuff." Lisa covered her eyes with her hand for a moment before emerging. "For some reason, I took his shame and made it my shame."

Michelle reached across the table to grab her hand. "I had no idea. I wish you would've said something."

Lisa took a sip of tea. "You know, I wish I had, too, but it took a long time. That's what shame does. It didn't hit me until I saw Justine's desperation written out like that, until I saw how shame and loneliness make all of us hide away..."

Val grabbed her other hand.

Lisa flashed a smile and took a deep breath. "We can't let our shame keep us apart, okay? We just can't."

"You're right, Lisa." Val broke her grasp, pulling away. "And I'm happy for you, but..."

A look of alarm crossed Lisa's face. "But what?"

"I feel partially responsible for this, like you're taking my advice in a way, and," Val blew out her lips, "I give *terrible* advice."

Lisa laughed, almost choking on a crumb of scone. "It wasn't you. Not really. You know, I never saw myself doing anything except cleaning up after him until the day I died. I thought I was doing what was best for him, and for the kids, and myself. I was wrong. If there's any chance of him getting better, he has to be away from me, as painful as that is." She stopped and smiled. "And now, I want to take Justine's advice. I want to dare to dream of another life."

Michelle felt like the air had gone out of her lungs. Lisa was a changed woman. "I'm happy for you," she finally managed to say.

"Thank you, but enough about me. Val, did your new album get picked up?"

Val shook her head. "Nah. I decided I've been clinging to that old version of myself for too long. I accepted the job at the university."

Lisa smacked her in the shoulder. "That's wonderful!"

"Ow!" Val smiled. "Thanks. I figure if my students are half as smart as Chloe, it'll be a good time."

Michelle beamed at her. "That's incredible, Val. You're going to be a great teacher."

She meant it. She wanted Val to be happy. She wanted Lisa to be happy. She even had given some thought to her own happiness recently.

The door popped open and Arthur appeared, as if tumbling out of her thoughts.

"Don't mind me," he said, pretending to shield his eyes. "Just dropping off these mushroom and garlic aioli tarts, in case anyone wanted them hot out of the oven."

"Thanks, Art," Michelle said. He winked at her before disappearing.

"So." Lisa crossed her arms. "Arthur's still around?"

Michelle stared down at her plate. "He is. We've started seeing each other and – "

She was cut off by Val and Lisa's squeals.

Oh well. She looked up and laughed at them. There was no use fighting it.

●●●

They gabbed on for hours and Michelle had to interrupt to talk about the tip she'd gotten earlier in the day. "A pod of resident orcas was spotted heading north from Puget Sound a few hours ago. They might be making their appearance here soon."

"Have they been back to the island yet this summer?" Lisa asked.

"No," Michelle shook her head. "Not yet. It may be a false alarm."

Val clapped her hands together. "Or maybe not! Let's get going. We can't miss their return!"

They got into Michelle's car and there wasn't a moment of silence until they pulled into the Lime Kiln State Park parking lot. Michelle was surprised to see it wasn't terribly busy, and there was a quiet peace amongst the trees.

They walked down the winding path into the park, past the grand Madrona trees, before spilling onto the rocky trail overlooking the ocean.

Michelle loved this view. It felt like the world opened up, the sea endless and vast.

They continued walking up the trail, excitement bubbling between them, until they got to the lighthouse and settled into a picnic table.

A group of twenty-something young women walked by, waving a hello. They waved back.

"Look, Val," Lisa said once they'd passed. "Your future students."

"Ha, I know. Impressionable young minds, huh?"

Speaking of impressionable young minds...

Michelle turned to her. "Are you still talking to Chloe?"

"I am." Val paused. "She's found some interesting information about Lou."

"Oh?" Michelle didn't want to encourage her, but on the other hand, she couldn't pretend she wasn't at all interested.

Val pulled her hat off and fluffed her hair. "I'm not going to drag you into it this time, but it seems Lou has some financial crimes to answer for."

"Financial?" Michelle paused. "How many homes will you need to break into to prove this?"

"None," Val said with a laugh. "I can tell you about it later. Where are Justine's ashes? I don't want it to get too dark."

Michelle dropped the subject and pulled the urn from her bag. The three of them found a spot on the rocks, overlooking the water, and took a small handful of ashes.

"Love you, girl," Michelle said, throwing her handful into the sea.

"Always," Lisa added.

Val's handful was rapidly disappearing from her fingers. "And forever."

They were standing there, admiring how the sunlight danced on the water, when the first fin appeared on the horizon.

"Look!" Michelle called out. "There they are!"

She ran back to the table and dug out her binoculars, handing them off to Val.

"I don't see anything!" she whined. "It's just water. I don't see where – wait!" She jumped up and down. "There! I see four of them!"

"They're coming right at us!" Lisa yelled.

Michelle wanted to say something, but it felt like her throat was swollen. She forced herself to take a deep breath.

Soon they didn't need binoculars. The entire pod meandered right up to shore, relaxed and having fun. They jumped, spyhopped, and smacked their tails onto the water. One of the young calves was tangling herself in kelp, playfully draping it over her body and flinging it into the air with her tail. She got so close that Michelle let out a yelp of glee.

Before long, the orcas passed by, and the three of them took their seats at the picnic table as the sun continued its glorious descent.

It had been a good day after all.

Thirty

Lou was in desperate need of money to fend off his creditors, so he was in a hurry, and they had to act fast. He'd planned an enormous fundraising event in Portland on Labor Day weekend, dubbing it "The Fall Revival." He claimed it was a place for Emeralds old and new to come together, learn, and grow.

In reality, the old Emeralds were required to bring at least two new attendees with them, or risk being labeled as "selfish" and "unwilling to share their knowledge of the journey."

Chloe explained this was a serious problem for indebted Emeralds. They could lose their chance to guide sessions in the future, and no sessions meant no way to erase debt they'd accumulated from attending their own sessions.

Quite a convenient arrangement – for Lou.

As per usual, the only paid employees at the event would be Lou's security team. Everyone else was expected to volunteer out of the goodness of their hearts – which, in Emerald terms, meant the fear in their souls – and not complain.

This was a detestable practice, but it did provide an opportunity. The Fall Revival was the largest Emerald event on the West Coast in over a decade, and finding volunteers on short notice proved to be difficult. Lou wouldn't even pay for the entertainment, saying that performers should be "banging down the doors for this kind of exposure."

Val told Lisa and Michelle about her plan, but unlike before, she didn't pressure them to participate. She admitted it had holes, and for that reason, she had mitigating strategies to avoid being trapped in a windowless room for a day.

They all had a good laugh, then Michelle announced she was going to help.

Lisa had been shocked when she heard it. Michelle hadn't even hesitated. She said this was the sort of thing she could get behind, helping people who had been exploited by Lou. If Chloe's optimistic hopes came true, then the entire community would be rid of Lou and his manipulative ways.

Lisa was more hesitant to sign up. Though she thought the idea had legs, she needed to focus on her new job. After Val debuted the idea at dinner the night after they had seen the whales, Lisa wished them luck, but went back home without making any promises.

It didn't last long. As soon as she mentioned Val's scheme to Sierra and Avery, it took off. Both of them had friends who'd been sucked into the Emerald Life, and they, too, wanted to help.

So, really, Lisa had no choice. On that picturesque Saturday in September, she found herself smack-dab in the middle of The Fall Revival.

It was being held in an enormous field, a popular spot for festivals, and there was plenty of room for the thousand-plus expected attendees. Lisa was stationed in the crowd, walking the grounds and watching for suspicious activity.

It wasn't a bad job. There were lots of people to watch and many sights to see. So many of the bright young faces reminded her of Justine. How many shared her genuine love of people, her joy for living? How much had Lou managed to take from each of them? A thousand dollars? Five thousand?

The space was abuzz with optimism. Music blasted as people moved between the dozens of booths – some for food and drinks, others for games and caricature drawings. The busiest booths were for Emerald session sign-ups and merchandise.

Near the back of the field, they'd set up a large stage with a jumbo TV and lights. Porta potties lined the outskirts, and since Lou was cheap and thought himself above regulations, there were only fifteen total, leading to long lines and an intense smell.

No one complained, though, as it wasn't the Emerald way. Lisa carried on, combing through the crowds, watching the security team and laying low.

This time, she had a disguise. Val had lent her a long, blonde wig and a wide-brimmed tan hat. She'd worn a summer dress Sierra had picked out and, to her delight, she seemed to blend in with the average twenty-something attendee, at least from behind. No one gave her a second glance. It was brilliant.

At noon, when the sun had reached its peak and the smell from the toilets was nearly unbearable, Lou made his entrance, running onto the stage to upbeat music. The crowd yelled and screamed, welcoming him, and confetti poured in from above.

When the noise died down, Lou yelled into the microphone. "I want to congratulate everyone here today."

More screams. They were treating him like a rock star.

Lisa took a few steps back. People were rushing to get closer and she didn't want to get swept up to the front.

"By being here today, you are taking the first steps to self-actualization! Give yourselves a round of applause!"

Blah.

For the next half hour, Lisa had to periodically look down at her feet as Lou droned on and on, saying words saturated with enthusiasm, but without any substance.

Finally, he passed the microphone off to one of his many volunteers and ran off stage.

Lisa watched him emerge, surrounded by security, and be whisked away to the VIP tent.

Perfect. She sent a text to the group. "On schedule."

The woman onstage waved a dramatic hand and spoke into the microphone. "Lou Emerald, everyone!"

The crowd cheered, and she nodded, a smile frozen on her face. Lisa thought she could make out a glint of terror in her eyes.

She was one of theirs. An Emerald who had crossed the line.

"You'll hear more about our sessions from Lou later," she said, her voice echoing. "Next up, we've got some music to kick off the day!"

She ran off and the lights dropped. A moment later, the stage erupted with brilliant shooting flames so bright that it blinded Lisa, forcing her to look away. When she looked again, a woman had emerged from the darkness, dressed head-to-toe in a white pantsuit, bedazzles throwing the light on her shoulders.

The first chords of *I Won't Be Bringing Home the Bacon Anymore* rang out, and the crowd went wild for Valerie Villano.

● ● ●

Michelle adjusted her headset. As the manager of the Heartfelt Tenderhooks, she had access to everything backstage and she was trying to keep her cool so she didn't mess up.

A text came in from Lisa. "No sight of him, no movement from the VIP tent. We have a minute, maybe?"

She clicked her microphone on and spoke. "Let's give Val thirty seconds before we send her the signal."

Kelly, the event coordinator, responded immediately. "Got it."

Michelle had liked Kelly from the moment they'd met. She had a loud, booming voice and a cackling laugh. After an introduction through Chloe, Kelly told her all about her first Emerald session eleven years prior. She'd lost her two-year-old daughter in a car crash and her entire world had crumbled.

A friend had dragged her to an Emerald event. That was when she'd met Justine. That was when things changed. Justine showed up at her door every day for the next three months, forcing her to go to coffee, dinner, ice cream – anything to keep her moving. Justine introduced her to other Emeralds, and slowly, Kelly made friends.

She attended all of the free Emerald sessions, and though she wasn't sold on the whole thing, she did think it gave her something to look forward to. No one judged her there, and she felt like she had a path to a new life.

That was the precise moment when Lou convinced her to take four thousand dollars' worth of sessions. She didn't have the money, but Lou had generously allowed her to take Emerald credit to pay back later.

Now, after years of leading her own sessions and volunteering at events, she only owed seven thousand and three hundred dollars, thanks to the interest she'd accrued.

The music cut out and Val's voice boomed through the speakers. "How are you all doing today?"

Cheers erupted from the audience.

"What a crowd!" Val beamed and blew a kiss. "Some of you might know me, but most of you probably don't. I'm Valerie Villano, and Justine Emerald was one of my dearest friends."

Michelle held her breath as a slow chaos rumbled through the staff. The people around her clutched their headsets. They started talking quickly and running off in different directions.

The timer had started.

She ran to the computer connected to the jumbo TV. The venue had recommended a more sophisticated system, but since Lou was unwilling to pay, he'd ended up with whatever the Heartfelt Tenderhooks had brought along with them.

Sucker.

The guy manning the computer had taken off, summoned by Kelly as per the plan. Michelle stared at the screen, out of breath and hands shaking.

She let the tension out of her shoulders and told herself to focus. Just as she'd practiced, she clicked over to the video Sierra had created for them and hit play.

"Is the video up?" she texted Lisa.

"Yes," she wrote back, "but there's no sound."

Shoot.

Michelle fiddled with the computer, but she was afraid to touch any of the cables. Maybe it was a broken setting?

Val's voice carried on. "Dear, sweet Justine is gone now, but I can see her spirit is living on through all of you. But, oh my, has Lou been a naughty boy!"

Another message from Lisa. "Security is on the move. Time to run!"

Michelle's muscles tensed. She wasn't going to be able to fix the sound. She ran to the edge of the stage and saw that the TV had big, bold captions, just as Sierra had promised.

That would have to do. She clicked her headset on. "Tell Val we have to go."

Kelly responded a second later. "You got it."

Val was still on the microphone, talking quickly. "Where does all the money go these days? Well, funny you asked – "

She stopped talking and looked straight at Michelle, who was waving her arms and mouthing, "We have to go!"

Val nodded and ran off stage, microphone still in hand. "The video you're seeing now is evidence unearthed by Emerald members showing what Lou has been up to, siphoning money from the company to line his own pockets. He's corrupted the Emerald mission, all in the name of greed."

They made it backstage to the hidden corner where Michelle had stashed a duffel bag. She tore the bag open and handed a wig, hat, and jacket to Val.

Val was still on the microphone, somehow getting changed without sounding out of breath in the least. "Have you ever felt pressured to bring in family or friends to sessions? Or to spend more money than you had?"

A few cheers from the crowd.

Val talked on as she slipped into the black leather jacket. "Know you're not alone. It doesn't have to be this way. Your pursuit of self-improvement doesn't make you weak. It means you're a good person, like Justine. And – "

The microphone went dead.

"Dang!" Val yelled, tossing the mic to the ground. "I was on a roll."

"You did amazing!" Michelle was already sweating under her furry coat and fiery red wig. She was seriously impressed Val managed to keep talking that whole time. "It's time to run!"

● ● ●

Val laughed. This was a thrill. This was *joy*.

She ran after Michelle and popped a pair of fake teeth into her mouth, slowing her pace only when a pair of security guys approached.

Michelle knelt down, pretending to fuss with a speaker. "What was that?" she whispered.

"Fake dentures," Val responded with a slight lisp. She knelt down, too, and a moment later, the security guys rushed by.

Michelle took off and Val followed.

What a day. Val loved that they'd pulled one over on Lou. She loved his team turning against him, and she'd loved her time on stage. Most of all, she loved being able to say Justine's name in front of all those people.

They weaved through the crowd, which was decidedly more disgruntled than before. Michelle led the way to the drink stand and they nearly ran into Lisa.

"I thought you were a teenager," Val yelled over the growing boos of the crowd.

Lisa winked at her. "Thanks, babe. It's all in the dress. Loved the show, by the way. Wish it could've gone longer."

Val laughed, then coughed, out of breath for the first time.

Michelle grabbed them and pulled them toward the exit. "Our ride's here."

Outside, past the booths and the stinking toilets, Arthur was waiting in a minivan. The doors were wide open. "Get in!" he yelled.

Val had campaigned for something flashier, faster, something fun. Michelle wouldn't budge, though, so here they were in their forest green escape van.

They piled in, Michelle pulling the doors shut, and off they went, cackling with laughter.

One year later

T hanks to Arthur's connections, they'd managed to snag a rental house on the west side of San Juan Island at a bargain price. The couple who owned the house used it as a vacation home, but they were far too busy to spend much time there during the year. They were happy to rent it to their favorite baker and his friends for a week that summer.

It was less like a house and more like a San Juan estate. Tucked away on a humble nine acres, the home overlooked Haro Strait and provided clear views of all passing orca pods. In the mornings, all they could hear were birds. In the evenings, the sunsets were brilliant and bold.

The main house had six bedrooms, four bathrooms, and two kitchens. The basement had an indoor pool where one of the glass walls opened fully to the outside in warmer months.

The other two homes on the property were quaintly called "cottages" because they only had three bedrooms apiece. A six-car garage was a fourth structure, complete with a workshop and yoga studio.

The estate had perfectly landscaped grounds woven together with walking paths and gardens, all expertly designed to conserve rainwater and prevent erosion.

Val, Lisa, and Michelle opted to stay in the big house together for the week. Their kids even managed to stop by for part of the week, though they chose to occupy the cottages. Tyler had brought his girlfriend Eliza, who was a delight, and Sierra and Avery came as a bickering pair.

Arthur came along, of course, and he tended to Michelle most diligently. Lisa brought her boyfriend Steve, a guy she'd met on a dating website. He was laugh-out-loud funny and worked as a systems analyst at lululemon.

He loved lululemon almost as much as he loved Lisa. Coincidentally, when he showered Michelle and Val with free lululemon leggings, tops, and jackets, they felt like they might love him, too.

Val didn't bring a guest, but she made sure to point out that no one should feel bad for her. "I've been so busy at the university! You wouldn't believe it. To be honest, my dating life has never been better."

"I hope you're not dating any of the students," Michelle said, serious faced.

Val was horrified at the mere suggestion. "Oh my gosh, no. I would never. It's unsettling, actually, how some of the kids have a strange reverence for me. I feel like...I don't know."

Lisa poked her. "What?"

"Like..." she shrugged. "Like I need to live up to their expectations."

"That's a good way to feel," Michelle said.

"It is." Val tossed her hair back and smiled mischievously. "Why do you ask, Shell? I hope none of your professors have tried to make a move on you."

Arthur shot her a mockingly alarmed look and Michelle laughed. "No, of course not." She rolled her eyes. "I've been very lucky. All of my professors are focused and dedicated, and they even got me connected to volunteer with the Orca Institute here. I'm officially helping catalog the orca pods and surveying their health and food supplies."

Lisa tapped her chin. "So you're scooping whale poop out of the water?"

Michelle nodded. "When I'm lucky, yes."

The air remained free of wildfire smoke, and the weather held magnificently for the entire week. Michelle managed to convince them to do a kayaking tour one day, which everyone enjoyed despite having to get their feet wet to launch their kayaks.

Sierra and Avery were able to join them for that, much to Lisa's delight. Less delightful were Avery's constant threats to tip the kayak. Luckily, he was bluffing and only intended to torture his sister. It worked.

To everyone's shock, Val suggested a bike ride the next day.

"I need to redeem myself," she said. After renting an e-bike, she kept up marvelously.

In the evenings, they sat out on the terrace under the twinkling lights, joking and laughing. The end of the week came too quickly, and on Saturday, they packed up the house and headed to the mainland.

They had to take a seaplane, much to Michelle's chagrin, but the flight was short and offered beautiful views of the islands. Once in Seattle, they met up with Chloe and the remaining Emerald leaders for a celebration.

Lou had just been sentenced for his extensive fraud. He was going to serve ten years, but that wasn't why they were celebrating.

Chloe and Kelly had spearheaded the rescue of the Emerald community, and they had been quite successful. They did away with expensive sessions and instead focused on what made the organization great to begin with: the community, and the earnest human effort towards trying to improve, to make life more bearable, if not a tad bit easier.

They were able to eliminate much of the debt fellow Emeralds had accumulated, and paid for others through restitution from Lou. In the end, they had a thriving community of people who supported each other, which is exactly what Justine would have wanted.

Chloe had asked Lisa, Michelle, and Val to attend as guests of honor for the Emerald banquet that evening. It wasn't a lavish affair – much humbler than what Lou would've put together – but there were drinks, a taco truck, and music.

Best of all was the unveiling of the Justine Emerald Fund. The money was reserved to help anyone down on their luck, whether it be to help pay for childcare, school, or a deposit on an apartment.

Michelle joked that the three of them were the first recipients of the fund, and their trip was the first disbursement.

"That's actually sort of true," Lisa said.

Val scoffed. "We were definitely not the most deserving candidates."

"No, maybe not." Michelle smiled. "Still. Justine brought us together again."

"She did," Lisa said with a heavy sigh.

Val grabbed each of them by the hand. "Now let's promise never to mess it up again!"

She pulled them to the dance floor without any protests. That evening, they danced, sang karaoke, and carried on into the wee hours of the morning. They were the last ones at the banquet, leaving only when the sun threatened to break into the horizon.

They made their way back to San Juan Island on an early ferry, braving the cool morning air to admire the stunning orange and pink skies from the deck. The three of them stood quietly, silent not from anger, but from the understanding that comes only once everything has been said.

Even in death, Justine had managed the impossible: she had reunited them, strengthened them, and inspired them to rise, rise again.

Would you like to join my reader group?

Looking for more adventure on the San Juan Islands? Join Amelia's reader group and get a free copy of Christmas at Saltwater Cove, a romance set on San Juan Island. You can sign up by visiting: https://bit.ly/XmasSWC

About the Author

Amelia Addler writes always sweet, always swoon-worthy romance stories and believes that everyone deserves their own happily ever after.

Her soulmate is a man who once spent five weeks driving her to work at 4AM after her car broke down (and he didn't complain, not even once). She is lucky enough to be married to that man and they live in Pittsburgh with their little yellow mutt. Visit her website at AmeliaAddler.com or drop her an email at amelia@AmeliaAddler.com.

Also by Amelia...

The Orcas Island Series

Sunset Cove

Sunset Secrets

Sunset Tides

The Westcott Bay Series

Saltwater Cove

Saltwater Studios

Saltwater Secrets

Saltwater Crossing

Saltwater Falls

Saltwater Memories

Saltwater Promises

Christmas at Saltwater Cove

Standalone Novels

The Summer Request

Made in the USA
Las Vegas, NV
22 June 2022

50584472R00156